STANDARD
LOAN

UNLESS RECALLED BY ANOTHER READER
THIS ITEM MAY BE BORROWED FOR
FOUR WEEKS

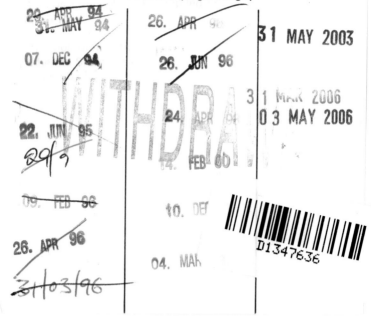

Longman

ST/GHO

FEB 1994

Contents

	page
An Introduction by Susan Hill	1
The Shadow-Cage Philippa Pearce	5
On the Brighton Road Richard Middleton	25
If She Bends, She Breaks John Gordon	31
The July Ghost A S Byatt	49
The Red Room H G Wells	71
Andrina George Mackay Brown	85
A Kind of Swan Song Helen Cresswell	97
The Man Who Didn't Believe in Ghosts Sorche Nic Leodhas	111
The Darkness under the Stairs Lance Salway	121
The Sea Bride Vivien Alcock	139
Points for Discussion and Suggestions for Writing	157
Wider Reading	164
Acknowledgements	168

An Introduction by Susan Hill

Ask anyone if they can tell you exactly what a ghost story is and the chances are that they will give you an account of quite a few. Browse along the bookshelves of your local library, or among the new fiction in a bookshop and you will find a lot of them, too; or rather, you will think you have found ghost stories. But look more closely. Many of them, like many that people will eagerly tell you about, will not be true ghost stories at all. They will be tales of horror or terror, or the uncanny and supernatural – perhaps, tales of the unexpected, the title of Roald Dahl's famous series. But none of these are what I mean by pure, traditional, classic ghost stories. All that they *must* have is a ghost, or at least, a 'haunting', of some kind. By 'ghost', I mean what is left – call it ghost, spirit or what you like – of someone who once lived in this world and who has died but who remains, or returns and is seen, heard, felt or sensed, by people still living in the here and now. Obviously, if this happens, it is generally 'unexpected' and may well be frightening and alarming. Nevertheless, not all ghosts have to be terrifying, evil or dreadful: and not all ghost stories either. That is what is wrong with so many written nowadays. The writers assume that to make an impact, a ghost story *has* to be terrifying, and that there has not only to be a ghost but a violent ghost, scenes of brutality, murders, and a lot of blood.

But ghost stories can be gentle, sad, tender, as well

1

as frightening – they can even be funny. We can feel sorry for the ghosts, and moved by the stories they have to tell. The mood of a ghost story can be mysterious, strange, eerie – odd – but although we will probably often shiver when reading it, we need not necessarily *shudder*.

One thing a ghost story *must* have is atmosphere – above all, the ghost story writer must conjure up the atmosphere of a particular place and mood and time, otherwise the story will not work. But not every short story has to have the classic ingredients that go to make up one kind of atmosphere – a dark, isolated, empty house, fog or a howling wind outside, flickering candles, strange footsteps . . . though of course it may incorporate all of these things.

It may be simply an entertainment, a clever piece of writing which one can admire for the way the tension is carefully built up, the gripping description which so cleverly conjures up the atmosphere of a place, the strange story of a haunting.

But there can be much more to the ghost story than this. A S Byatt's beautiful and very moving story, *The July Ghost*, is about the nature of grief and the long-term psychological and emotional effects upon a woman of the death of her beloved child in sudden and tragic circumstances. It is a poignant story which raises all sorts of questions, and I find it hauntingly beautiful – but it is not in the least bit frightening.

Study of the ghost story is a study, so often, of excellent writing. Many of the greatest authors have turned their hand to the form – Oscar Wilde, Henry James, Kipling, Charles Dickens, H G Wells. And in one sense, you could say that Shakespeare's *Hamlet* is just one of the best ghost stories ever written – in dramatic form.

But when you have read the story and been chilled or moved by it, when you have analysed how cleverly the author makes use of the essential ingredients, evokes atmosphere and creates and builds up tension and brings about a dénouement – then you are left with other, even deeper matters. The ghost story raises all manner of important questions.

It leads inevitably to discussion of the basic question 'Do *you* believe in ghosts?' which is actually a very serious one, involving questions about the very nature of human life, the personality and death. What *is* a human being? What is 'mind', 'brain', 'personality', 'spirit'? Can or does any of this survive after death? How? What? If so, what has this to do with this world, here and now, and us? What has it to do with God and religion? What would a 'ghost' be? *Why* would it haunt? What bearing has any of this on how we behave and what we are and hope to become, here and now? Or is it all just a fantasy? Just stories? If so, why? What are the likely explanations of the many accounts of ghosts and hauntings? Why would people imagine they had seen a ghost? If they had not and were lying, why? What about telepathy? Poltergeists? Spiritualists and mediums?

What a lot of topics to be thought about and discussed! And what a lot of marvellous ghost stories there are to read. (And what a lot of awful ones, too – and that's another whole area for study and discussion: comparisons between well-written, even great, ghost stories, and trashy ones.)

I hope the stories collected here will be enjoyable, entertaining and thought-provoking. I hope you will admire their variety and their different atmosphere and backgrounds, and that they will give you an idea of what a good and serious literary form the ghost story can be, and perhaps put it in a new light, too, as something rather different from what you had perhaps previously assumed it to be – just a lot of shrieks and spooks to give you nightmares – or even, make you laugh at some of the far-fetched atmospherics. Ghost stories are much more, much better, than that.

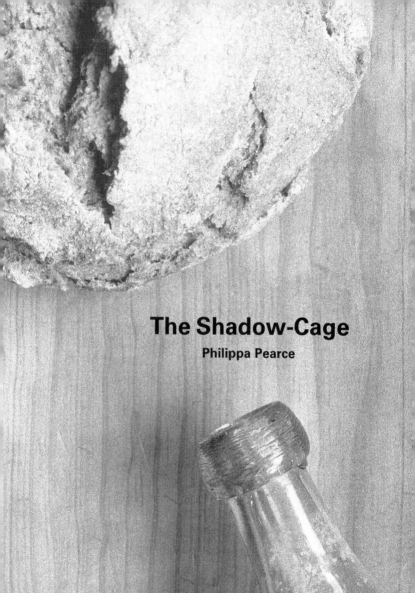

The Shadow-Cage

Philippa Pearce

Philippa Pearce

The Shadow-Cage

The little green stoppered bottle had been waiting in the earth for a long time for someone to find it. Ned Challis found it. High on his tractor as he ploughed the field, he'd been keeping a look-out, as usual, for whatever might turn up. Several times there had been worked flints; once, one of an enormous size.

Now sunlight glimmering on glass caught his eye. He stopped the tractor, climbed down, picked the bottle from the earth. He could tell at once that it wasn't all that old. Not as old as the flints that he'd taken to the museum in Castleford. Not as old as a coin he had once found, with the head of a Roman emperor on it. Not very old; but old.

Perhaps just useless old . . .

He held the bottle in the palm of his hand and thought of throwing it away. The lip of it was chipped badly, and the stopper of cork or wood had sunk into the neck. With his fingernail he tried to move it. The stopper had hardened into stone, and stuck · there. Probably no one would ever get it out now without breaking the bottle. But then, why should anyone want to unstopper the bottle? It was empty, or as good as empty. The bottom of the inside of the bottle was dirtied with something blackish and scaly that also clung a little to the sides.

He wanted to throw the bottle away, but he didn't. He held it in one hand while the fingers of the other cleaned the remaining earth from the outside. When he had cleaned it, he didn't fancy the bottle any more than before; but he dropped it into his pocket. Then he climbed the tractor and started off again.

At that time the sun was high in the sky, and the tractor was working on Whistlers' Hill, which is part of Belper's Farm, fifty yards below Burnt House. As the tractor moved on again, the gulls followed again, rising and falling in their flights, wheeling over the disturbed earth, looking for live things, for food; for good things.

That evening, at tea, Ned Challis brought the bottle out and set it on the table by the loaf of bread. His wife looked at it suspiciously: 'Another of your dirty old things for that museum?'

Ned said: 'It's not museum-stuff. Lisa can have it to take to school. I don't want it.'

Mrs Challis pursed her lips, moved the loaf further away from the bottle, and went to refill the tea-pot.

Lisa took the bottle in her hand. 'Where'd you get it, Dad?'

'Whistlers' Hill. Just below Burnt House.' He frowned suddenly as he spoke, as if he had remembered something.

'What's it got inside?'

'Nothing. And if you try getting the stopper out, that'll break.'

So Lisa didn't try. Next morning she took it to school; but she didn't show it to anyone. Only her cousin Kevin saw it, and that was before school and by accident. He always called for Lisa on his way to school – there was no other company on that country road – and saw her pick up the bottle from the table, where her mother had left it the night before, and put it into her anorak pocket.

'What was that?' asked Kevin.

'You saw. A little old bottle.'

'Let's see it again – properly.' Kevin was younger than Lisa, and she sometimes indulged him; so she took the bottle out and let him hold it.

At once he tried the stopper.

'Don't,' said Lisa. 'You'll only break it.'

'What's inside?'

'Nothing. Dad found it on Whistlers'.'

'It's not very nice, is it?'

'What do you mean, "Not very nice"?'

'I don't know. But let me keep it for a bit. Please, Lisa.'

On principle Lisa now decided not to give in. 'Certainly not. Give it back.'

He did, reluctantly. 'Let me have it just for today, at school. Please.'

'No.'

'I'll give you something if you'll let me have it. I'll not let anyone else touch it; I'll not let them see it. I'll keep it safe. Just for today.'

'You'd only break it. No. What could you give me, anyway?'

'My week's pocket-money.'

'No. I've said no and I mean no, young Kev.'

'I'd give you that little china dog you like.'

'The one with the china kennel?'

'Yes.'

'The china dog with the china kennel – you'd give me both?'

'Yes.'

'Only for half the day, then,' said Lisa. 'I'll let you have it after school-dinner – look out for me in the playground. Give it back at the end of school. Without fail. And you be careful with it.'

So the bottle travelled to school in Lisa's anorak pocket. where it bided its time all morning. After school-dinner Lisa met Kevin in the playground and they withdrew together to a corner which was well away from the crowded climbing-frame and the infants' sandpit and the rest. Lisa handed the bottle over. 'At the end of school, mind, without fail. And if we miss each other then,' – for Lisa, being in a higher class, came out of school slightly later than Kevin – 'then you must drop it in at ours as you pass. Promise.'

'Promise.'

They parted. Kevin put the bottle into his pocket. He didn't know why he'd wanted the bottle, but he had. Lots of things were like that. You needed them for a bit; and then you didn't need them any longer.

He had needed this little bottle very much.

He left Lisa and went over to the climbing-frame, where his friends already were. He had set his foot on a rung when he thought suddenly how easy it would be for the glass bottle in his trouser pocket to be smashed against the metal framework. He stepped down again and went over to the fence that separated the playground from the farmland beyond. Tall tussocks of grass grew along it, coming through from the open fields and fringing the very edge of the asphalt. He looked round: Lisa had already gone in, and no one else was watching. He put his hand into his pocket and took it out again with the bottle concealed in the fist. He stooped as if to examine an insect on a tussock, and slipped his hand into the middle of it and left the bottle there, well hidden.

He straightened up and glanced around. Since no one was looking in his direction, his action had been unob-served; the bottle would be safe. He ran back to the climbing-frame and began to climb, jostling and shouting and laughing, as he and his friends always did. He forgot the bottle.

He forgot the bottle completely.

It was very odd, considering what a fuss he had made about the bottle, that he should have forgotten it; but he did. When the bell rang for the end of playtime, he ran straight in. He did not think of the bottle then, or later. At the end of the afternoon school, he did not remember it; and he happened not to see Lisa, who would surely have reminded him.

Only when he was nearly home, and passing the Challises' house, he remembered. He had faithfully promised – and had really meant to keep his promise. But he'd broken it, and left the bottle behind. If he turned and went back to school now, he would meet Lisa, and she would have to be told . . . By the time he got back to the school playground, all his friends would have gone home: the caretaker would be there, and perhaps a late teacher or two, and they'd all want to know what he was up to. And when he'd got the bottle and dropped it in at the Challises', Lisa would scold him all over again. And when he got home at last, he would be very late for his tea, and his mother would be angry.

As he stood by the Challises' gate, thinking, it seemed best, since he had messed things up anyway, to go straight home and leave the bottle to the next day. So he went home.

He worried about the bottle for the rest of the day, without having the time or the quiet to think about it very clearly. He knew that Lisa would assume he had just forgotten to leave it at her house on the way home. He half expected her to turn up after tea, to claim it; but she didn't. She would have been angry enough about his having forgotten to leave it; but what about her anger tomorrow on the way to school, when she found that he had forgotten it altogether – abandoned it in the open playground? He thought of hurrying straight past her house in the morning; but he would never manage it. She would be on the look-out.

He saw that he had made the wrong decision earlier. He ought, at all costs, to have gone back to the playground to get the bottle.

He went to bed, still worrying. He fell asleep, and his worry went on, making his dreaming unpleasant in a nagging way. He must be quick, his dreams seemed to nag. *Be quick . . .*

Suddenly he was wide awake. It was very late. The sound of the television being switched off must have woken him. Quietness. He listened to the rest of his family going to bed. They went to bed and to sleep. Silence. They were all asleep now, except for him. He couldn't sleep.

Then, as abruptly as if someone had lifted the top of his head like a lid and popped the idea in, he saw that this time – almost the middle of the night – was the perfect time for him to fetch the bottle. He knew by heart the roads between home and school; he would not be afraid. He would have plenty of time. When he reached the school, the gate to the playground would be shut, but it was not high: in the past, by daylight, he and his friends had often climbed it. He would go into the playground, find the correct tussock of grass, get the bottle, bring it back, and have it ready to give to Lisa on the way to school in the morning. She would be angry, but only moderately angry. She would never know the whole truth.

He got up and dressed quickly and quietly. He began to look for a pocket-torch, but gave up when he realised that would mean opening and shutting drawers and cupboards. Anyway, there was a moon tonight, and he knew his way, and he knew the school playground. He couldn't go wrong.

He let himself out of the house, leaving the door on the latch for his return. He looked at his watch: between a quarter and half past eleven – not as late as he had thought. All the same, he set off almost at a run, but had to settle down to a steady trot. His trotting footsteps on the road sounded clearly in the night quiet. But who was there to hear?

He neared the Challises' house. He drew level with it.

Ned Challis heard. Usually nothing woke him before the alarm-clock in the morning; but tonight footsteps woke him. Who, at this hour – he lifted the back of his wrist towards his face, so that the time glimmered at him – who, at nearly twenty-five to twelve, could be hurrying along that road on foot? When the footsteps had almost gone – when it was already perhaps too late he sprang out of bed and over to the window.

His wife woke. 'What's up, then, Ned?'

'Just somebody. I wondered who.'

'Oh, come back to bed!'

Ned Challis went back to bed; but almost at once got out again.

'Ned! What is it now?'

'I just thought I'd have a look at Lisa.'

At once Mrs Challis was wide awake. 'What's wrong with Lisa?'

'Nothing.' He went to listen at Lisa's door – listen to the regular, healthy breathing of her sleep. He came back. 'Nothing. Lisa's all right.'

'For heavens' sake! Why shouldn't she be?'

'Well, who was it walking out there? Hurrying.'

'Oh, go to sleep!'

'Yes.' He lay down again, drew the bedclothes round him, lay still. But his eyes remained open.

Out in the night, Kevin left the road on which the Challises lived and came into the more important one that would take him into the village. He heard the rumble of a lorry coming up behind him. For safety he drew right into a gateway and waited. The lorry came past at a steady pace, headlights on. For a few seconds he saw the driver and his mate sitting up in the cab, intent on the road ahead. He had not wanted to be noticed by them, but, when they had gone, he felt lonely.

He went on into the village, its houses lightless, its streets deserted. By the entrance to the school driveway, he stopped to make sure he was unobserved. Nobody. Nothing – not even a cat. There was no sound of any vehicle now; but in the distance he heard a dog barking, and then another answered it. A little owl cried and cried for company or for sport. Then that, too, stopped.

He turned into the driveway to the school, and there was the gate to the playground. He looked over it, into the playground. Moonlight showed him everything: the expanse of asphalt, the sandpit, the big climbing-frame, and – at the far end – the fence with the tussocks of grass growing blackly along it. It was all familiar, and yet strange because of the emptiness and the whitening of moonlight and the shadows cast like solid things. The climbing-frame reared high into the air, and on the ground stretched the black criss-cross of its shadows like the bars of a cage.

But he had not come all this way to be halted by moonshine and insubstantial shadows. In a businesslike way he climbed the gate and crossed the playground to the fence. He wondered whether he would find the right tussock easily, but he did. His fingers closed on the bottle: it was waiting for him.

At that moment, in the Challises' house, as they lay side by side in bed, Mrs Challis said to her husband: 'You're still awake, aren't you?'

'Yes.'

'What is it?'

'Nothing.'

Mrs Challis sighed.

'All right, then,' said Ned Challis. 'It's this. That bottle I gave Lisa — that little old bottle that I gave Lisa yesterday —'

'What about it?'

'I found it by Burnt House.'

Mrs Challis drew in her breath sharply. Then she said, 'That may mean nothing.' Then, 'How near was it?'

'Near enough.' After a pause: 'I ought never to have given it to Lisa. I never thought. But Lisa's all right, anyway.'

'But, Ned, don't you know what Lisa did with that bottle?'

'What?'

'Lent it to Kevin to have at school. And, according to her, he didn't return it when he should have done, on the way home. Didn't you hear her going on and on about it?'

'Kevin . . .' For the third time that night Ned Challis was getting out of bed, this time putting on his trousers, fumbling for his shoes. 'Somebody went up the road in a hurry. You know — I looked out. I couldn't see properly, but it was somebody small. It could have been a child. It could have been Lisa, but it wasn't. It could well have been Kevin . . .'

'Shouldn't you go to their house first, Ned — find out

whether Kevin is there or not? Make sure. You're not sure.'

'I'm not sure. But, if I wait to make sure, I may be too late.'

Mrs Challis did not say, 'Too late for what?' She did not argue.

Ned Challis dressed and went down. As he let himself out of the house to get his bicycle from the shed, the church clock began to strike the hour, the sound reaching him distantly across the intervening fields. He checked with his watch: midnight.

In the village, in the school playground, the striking of midnight sounded clangorously close. Kevin stood with the bottle held in the palm of his hand, waiting for the clock to stop striking – waiting as if for something to follow.

After the last stroke of midnight, there was silence, but Kevin still stood waiting and listening. A car or lorry passed the entrance of the school drive: he heard it distinctly; yet it was oddly faint, too. He couldn't place the oddness of it. It had sounded much further away than it should have done – less really there.

He gripped the bottle and went on listening, as if for some particular sound. The minutes passed. The same dog barked at the same dog, bark and reply – far, unreally far away. The little owl called; from another world, it might have been.

He was gripping the bottle so tightly now that his hand was sweating. He felt his skin begin to prickle with sweat at the back of his neck and under his arms.

Then there was a whistle from across the fields, distantly. It should have been an unexpected sound, just after midnight; but it did not startle him. It did set him off across the playground, however. Too late he wanted to get away. He had to go past the climbing-frame, whose cagework of shadows now stretched more largely than the frame itself. He saw the bars of shadows as he approached; he actually hesitated; and then, like a fool, he stepped inside the cage of shadows.

Ned Challis, on his bicycle, had reached the junction of the by-road with the road that – in one direction – led to the village. In the other it led deeper into the country. Which way? He dismounted. He had to choose the right way – to follow Kevin.

Thinking of Whistlers' Hill, he turned the front wheel of his bicycle away from the village and set off again. But now, with his back to the village, going away from the village, he felt a kind of weariness and despair. A memory of childhood came into his mind: a game he had played in childhood: something hidden for him to find, and if he turned in the wrong direction to search, all the voices whispered to him, 'Cold – cold!' Now, with the village receding behind him, he recognised what he felt: cold . . . cold . . .

Without getting off his bicycle, he wheeled round and began to pedal hard in the direction of the village.

In the playground, there was no pressing hurry for Kevin any more. He did not press against the bars of his cage to get out. Even when clouds cut off the moonlight and the shadows melted into general darkness – even when the shadow-cage was no longer visible to the eye, he stood there; then crouched there, in a corner of the cage, as befitted a prisoner.

The church clock struck the quarter.

The whistlers were in no hurry. The first whistle had come from right across the fields. Then there was a long pause. Then the sound was repeated, equally distantly, from the direction of the river bridges. Later still, another whistle from the direction of the railway line, or somewhere near it.

He lay in his cage, cramped by the bars, listening. He did not know he was thinking, but suddenly it came to him: Whistlers' Hill. He and Lisa and the others had always supposed that the hill had belonged to a family called Whistler, as Challises' house belonged to the Challis family. But that was not how the hill had got its name – he saw that now. No indeed not.

Whistler answered whistler at long intervals, like the sentries of a besieging army. There was no moving in as yet.

The church clock had struck the quarter as Ned Challis entered the village and cycled past the entrance to the school. He cycled as far as the Recreation Ground, perhaps because that was where Kevin would have gone in the daytime. He cycled bumpily round the Ground: no Kevin.

He began to cycle back the way he had come, as though he had given up altogether and was going home. He cycled slowly. He passed the entrance to the school again.

In this direction, he was leaving the village. He was cycling so slowly that the front wheel of his bicycle wobbled desperately; the light from his dynamo was dim. He put a foot down and stopped. Motionless, he listened. There was nothing to hear, unless – yes, the faintest ghost of a sound, high pitched, prolonged for seconds, remote as from another world. Like a coward – and Ned Challis was no coward – he tried to persuade himself that he had imagined the sound; yet he knew he had not. It came from another direction now: very faint, yet penetrating, so that his skin crinkled to hear it. Again it came, from yet another quarter.

He wheeled his bicycle back to the entrance to the school and left it there. He knew he must be very close. He walked up to the playground gate and peered over it. But the moon was obscured by cloud: he could see nothing. He listened, waited for the moon to sail free.

In the playground Kevin had managed to get up, first on his hands and knees, then upright. He was very much afraid, but he had to be standing to meet whatever it was.

For the whistlers had begun to close in slowly, surely: converging on the school, on the school playground, on the cage of shadows. On him.

For some time now cloud-masses had obscured the moon. He could see nothing; but he felt the whistlers' presence. Their signals came more often, and always closer. Closer. Very close.

Suddenly the moon sailed free.

In the sudden moonlight Ned Challis saw clear across the playground to where Kevin stood against the climbing-frame, with his hands writhing together in front of him.

In the sudden moonlight Kevin did not see his uncle. Between him and the playground gate, and all round him, air was thickening into darkness. Frantically he tried to undo his fingers, that held the little bottle, so that he could throw it from him. But he could not. He held the bottle; the bottle held him.

The darkness was closing in on him. The darkness was about to take him; had surely got him.

Kevin shrieked.

Ned Challis shouted: 'I'm here!' and was over the gate and across the playground and with his arms round the boy: '*I've got you.*'

There was a tinkle as something fell from between Kevin's opened fingers: the little bottle fell and rolled to the middle of the playground. It lay there, very insignificant-looking.

Kevin was whimpering and shaking, but he could move of his own accord. Ned Challis helped him over the gate and to the bicycle.

'Do you think you could sit on the bar, Kev? Could you manage that?'

'Yes.' He could barely speak.

Ned Challis hesitated, thinking of the bottle which had chosen to come to rest in the very centre of the playground, where the first child tomorrow would see it, pick it up.

He went back and picked the bottle up. Wherever he threw it, someone might find it. He might smash it and grind the pieces underfoot; but he was not sure he dared to do that.

Anyway, he was not going to hold it in his hand longer than he strictly must. He put it in his pocket, and then, when he got back to Kevin and the bicycle, he slipped it into the saddle-bag.

He rode Kevin home on the cross-bar of his bicycle. At the Challises' front gate Mrs Challis was waiting, with the dog for company. She just said: 'He all right then?'

'Ah?'

'I'll make a cup of tea while you take him home.'

At his own front door, Kevin said, 'I left the door on the latch. I can get in. I'm all right. I'd rather – I'd rather – '

'Less spoken of, the better,' said his uncle. 'You go to bed. Nothing to be afraid of now.'

He waited until Kevin was inside the house and he heard the latch click into place. Then he rode back to his wife, his cup of tea, and consideration of the problem that lay in his saddle-bag.

After he had told his wife everything, and they had discussed possibilities, Ned Challis said thoughtfully: 'I might take it to the museum, after all. Safest place for it would be inside a glass case there.'

'But you said they wouldn't want it.'

'Perhaps they would, if I told them where I found it and a bit – only a bit – about Burnt House...'

'You do that, then.'

Ned Challis stood up and yawned with a finality that said, Bed.

'But don't you go thinking you've solved all your problems by taking that bottle to Castleford, Ned. Not by a long chalk.'

'No?'

'Lisa. She reckons she owns that bottle.'

'I'll deal with Lisa tomorrow.'

'Today, by the clock.'

Ned Challis gave a groan that turned into another yawn. 'Bed first,' he said; 'then Lisa.' They went to bed not long before dawn.

The next day and for days after that, Lisa was furiously angry with her father. He had as good as stolen her bottle, she said, and now he refused to give it back, to let her see it, even to tell her what he had done with it. She was less angry with Kevin. (She did not know, of course, the circumstances of the bottle's passing from Kevin to her father.)

Kevin kept out of Lisa's way, and even more care-fully kept out of his uncle's. He wanted no private conversation.

One Saturday Kevin was having tea at the Challises', because he had been particularly invited. He sat with Lisa and Mrs Challis. Ned had gone to Castleford, and came in late. He joined them at the tea-table in evident good spirits. From his pocket he brought out a small cardboard box, which he placed in the centre of the table, by the Saturday cake. His wife was staring at him: before he spoke, he gave her the slightest nod of reassurance. 'The museum didn't want to keep that little old glass bottle, after all,' he said.

Both the children gave a cry: Kevin started up with such a violent backward movement that his chair clattered to the floor behind him; Lisa leant forward, her fingers clawing towards the box.

'No!' Ned Challis said. To Lisa he added: 'There it stays, girl, till *I* say.' To Kevin: 'Calm down. Sit up at the table again and listen to me.' Kevin picked his chair up and sat down again, resting his elbows on the table, so that his hands supported his head.

'Now,' said Ned Challis, 'you two know so much that it's probably better you should know more. That little old bottle came from Whistlers' Hill, below Burnt House – well, you know that. Burnt House is only a ruin now – elder bushes growing inside as well as out; but once it was a cottage that someone lived in. Your mother's granny remembered the last one to live there.'

'No, Ned,' said Mrs Challis, 'it was my great-granny remembered.'

'Anyway,' said Ned Challis, 'it was so long ago that Victoria was the Queen, that's certain. And an old woman lived alone in that cottage. There were stories about her.'

'Was she a witch?' breathed Lisa.

'So they said. They said she went out on the hillside at night –'

'At the full of the moon,' said Mrs Challis.

'They said she dug up roots and searched out plants and toadstools and things. They said she caught rats and toads and even bats. They said she made ointments and powders and weird brews. And they said she used what she made to cast spells and call up spirits.'

'Spirits from Hell, my great-granny said. Real bad 'uns.'

'So people said, in the village. Only the parson scoffed at the whole idea. Said he'd called often and been shown over the cottage and seen nothing out of the ordinary – none of the jars and bottles of stuff that she was supposed to have for her witchcraft. He said she was just a poor cranky old woman; that was all.

'Well, she grew older and older and crankier and crankier, and one day she died. Her body lay in its coffin in the cottage, and the parson was going to bury her next day in the churchyard.

'The night before she was to have been buried, someone went up from the village – '

'Someone!' said Mrs Challis scornfully. 'Tell them the whole truth, Ned, if you're telling the story at all. Half the village went up, with lanterns – men, women, and children. Go on, Ned.'

'The cottage was thatched, and they began to pull swatches of straw away and take it into the cottage and strew it round and heap it up under the coffin. They were going to fire it all.

'They were pulling the straw on the downhill side of the cottage when suddenly a great piece of thatch came away and out came tumbling a whole lot of things that the old woman must have kept hidden there. People did hide things in thatches, in those days.'

'Her savings?' asked Lisa.

'No. A lot of jars and little bottles, all stoppered or sealed, neat and nice. With stuff inside.'

There was silence at the tea-table. Then Lisa said: 'That proved it: she was a witch.'

'Well, no, it only proved she *thought* she was a witch. That was what the parson said afterwards – and whew! was he mad when he knew about that night.'

Mrs Challis said: 'He gave it 'em red hot from the pulpit the next Sunday. He said that once upon a time poor old deluded creatures like her had been burnt alive for no reason at all, and the village ought to be ashamed of having burnt her dead.'

Lisa went back to the story of the night itself. 'What did they do with what came out of the thatch?'

'Bundled it inside the cottage among the straw, and fired it all. The cottage burnt like a beacon that night, they say. Before cockcrow, everything had been burnt to ashes. That's the end of the story.'

'Except for my little bottle,' said Lisa. 'That came out of the thatch, but it didn't get picked up. It rolled downhill, or someone kicked it.'

'That's about it,' Ned agreed.

Lisa stretched her hand again to the cardboard box, and this time he did not prevent her. But he said: 'Don't be surprised, Lisa. It's different.'

She paused. 'A different bottle?'

'The same bottle, but – well, you'll see.'

Lisa opened the box, lifted the packaging of cotton wool, took the bottle out. It was the same bottle, but the stopper had gone, and it was empty and clean – so clean that it shone greenly. Innocence shone from it.

'You said the stopper would never come out,' Lisa said slowly.

'They forced it by suction. The museum chap wanted to know what was inside, so he got the hospital lab to take a look – he has a friend there. It was easy for them.'

Mrs Challis said: 'That would make a pretty vase, Lisa. For tiny flowers.' She coaxed Lisa to go out to pick a posy from the garden; she herself took the bottle away to fill it with water.

Ned Challis and Kevin faced each other across the table. Kevin said: 'What was in it?'

Ned Challis said: 'A trace of this, a trace of that, the hospital said. One thing more than anything else.'

'Yes?'

'Blood. Human blood.'

Lisa came back with her flowers; Mrs Challis came back with the bottle filled with water. When the flowers had been put in, it looked a pretty thing.

'My witch-bottle,' said Lisa contentedly. 'What was she called – the old woman that thought she was a witch?'

Her father shook his head; her mother thought: 'Madge – or was it Maggy?'

'Maggy Whistler's bottle, then,' said Lisa.

'Oh, no,' said Mrs Challis. 'She was Maggy – or Madge – Dawson. I remember my granny saying so. Dawson.

'Then why's it called Whistlers' Hill?'

'I'm not sure,' said Mrs Challis uneasily. 'I mean, I don't think anyone knows for certain.'

But Ned Challis, looking at Kevin's face, knew that he knew for certain.

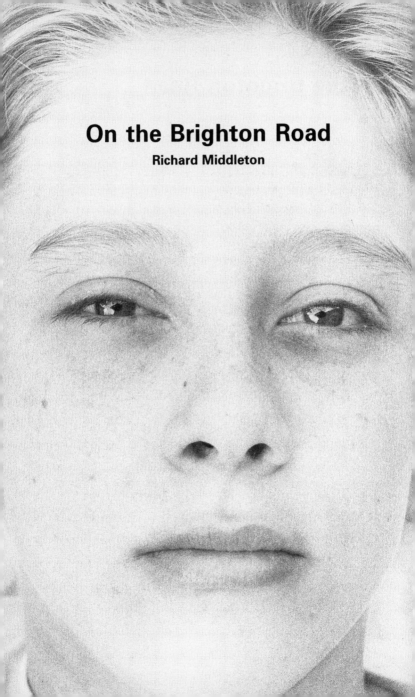

On the Brighton Road

Richard Middleton

Richard Middleton

On the Brighton Road

Slowly the sun had climbed up the hard white downs, till it broke with little of the mysterious ritual of dawn upon a sparkling world of snow. There had been a hard frost during the night, and the birds, who hopped about here and there with scant tolerance of life, left no trace of their passage on the silver pavements. In places the sheltered caverns of the hedges broke the monotony of the whiteness that had fallen upon the coloured earth, and overhead the sky melted from orange to deep blue, from deep blue to a blue so pale that it suggested a thin paper screen rather than illimitable space. Across the level fields there came a cold, silent wind which blew fine dust of snow from the trees, but hardly stirred the crested hedges. Once above the skyline, the sun seemed to climb more quickly, and as it rose higher it began to give out a heat that blended with the keenness of the wind.

It may have been this strange alternation of heat and cold that disturbed the tramp in his dreams, for he struggled for a moment with the snow that covered him, like a man who finds himself twisted uncomfortably in the bed-clothes, and then sat up with staring, questioning eyes. 'Lord! I thought I was in bed,' he said to himself as he took in the vacant landscape, 'and all the while I was out here.' He stretched his limbs, and rising carefully to his feet, shook the snow off his body. As he did so the wind set him shivering, and he knew that his bed had been warm.

'Come, I feel pretty fit,' he thought. 'I suppose I am lucky to wake at all in this. Or unlucky – it isn't much of a business to come back to.' He looked up and saw the downs shining against the blue like the Alps on a picture-postcard. 'That means another forty miles or so, I suppose,' he continued grimly. 'Lord knows what I did yesterday. Walked till I was done, and now I'm only about twelve miles from Brighton. Damn the snow, damn Brighton, damn everything!' The sun crept up higher and higher, and he started walking patiently along the road with his back turned to the hills.

'Am I glad or sorry that it was only sleep that took me, glad or sorry, glad or sorry?' His thoughts seemed to arrange themselves in a metrical accompaniment to the steady thud of his footsteps, and he hardly sought an answer to his question. It was good enough to walk to.

Presently, when three milestones had loitered past, he overtook a boy who was stooping to light a cigarette. He wore no overcoat, and looked unspeakably fragile against the snow. 'Are you on the road, guv 'nor?' asked the boy huskily as he passed.

'I think I am,' the tramp said.

'Oh! then I'll come a bit of the way with you if you don't walk too fast. It's a bit lonesome walking this time of day. 'The tramp nodded his head, and the boy started limping along by his side.

'I'm eighteen,' he said casually. 'I bet you thought I was younger.'

'Fifteen, I'd have said.'

'You'd have backed a loser. Eighteen last August, and I've been on the road six years. I ran away from home five times when I was a little 'un, and the police took me back each time. Very good to me, the police was. Now I haven't got a home to run away from.'

'Nor have I,' the tramp said calmly.

'Oh, I can see what you are,' the boy panted; 'you're a gentleman come down. It's harder for you than for me.' The tramp glanced at the limping, feeble figure and lessened his pace.

'I haven't been at it as long as you have,' he admitted.

'No, I could tell that by the way you walk. You haven't got tired yet. Perhaps you expect something the other end?'

The tramp reflected for a moment. 'I don't know,' he said bitterly. 'I'm always expecting things.'

'You'll grow out of that,' the boy commented. 'It's warmer in London, but it's harder to come by grub. There isn't much in it really.'

'Still, there's the chance of meeting somebody there who will understand —'

'Country people are better,' the boy interrupted. 'Last night I took a lease of a barn for nothing and slept with the cows, and this morning the farmer routed me out and gave me tea and toke because I was little. Of course, I score there; but in London, soup on the Embankment at night, and all the rest of the time coppers moving you on.'

'I dropped by the roadside last night and slept where I fell. It's a wonder I didn't die,' the tramp said. The boy looked at him sharply.

'How do you know you didn't? he said.

'I don't see it,' the tramp said, after a pause.

'I tell you,' the boy said hoarsely, 'people like us can't get away from this sort of thing if we want to. Always hungry and thirsty and dog-tired and walking all the time. And yet if anyone offers me a nice home and work my stomach feels sick. Do I look strong? I know I'm little for my age, but I've been knocking about like this for six years, and do you think I'm not dead? I was drowned bathing at Margate, and I was killed by a gipsy with a spike; he knocked my head right in, and twice I was froze like you last night, and a motor cut me down on this very road, and yet I'm walking along here now, walking to London to walk away from it again, because I can't help it. Dead! I tell you we can't get away if we want to.'

The boy broke off in a fit of coughing, and the tramp paused while he recovered.

'You'd better borrow my coat for a bit, Tommy,' he said, 'your cough's pretty bad.'

'You go to hell!' the boy said fiercely, puffing at his cigarette; 'I'm all right. I was telling you about the road. You haven't got down to it yet, but you'll find out presently. We're all dead, all of us who're on it, and we're all tired, yet somehow we can't leave it. There's nice smells in the summer, dust and hay and the wind smack in your face on a hot day; and it's nice waking up in the wet grass on a fine morning. I don't know, I don't know —' he lurched forward suddenly, and the tramp caught him in his arms.

'I'm sick,' the boy whispered — 'sick.'

The tramp looked up and down the road, but he could see no houses or any sign of help. Yet even as he supported the boy doubtfully in the middle of the road a motor-car suddenly flashed in the middle distance, and came smoothly through the snow.

'What's the trouble?' said the driver quietly as he pulled up. 'I'm a doctor.' He looked at the boy keenly and listened to his strained breathing.

'Pneumonia,' he commented. 'I'll give him a lift to the infirmary, and you, too, if you like.'

The tramp thought of the workhouse and shook his head. 'I'd rather walk,' he said.

The boy winked faintly as they lifted him into the car.

'I'll meet you beyond Reigate,' he murmured to the tramp. 'You'll see.' And the car vanished along the white road.

All the morning the tramp splashed through the thawing snow, but at midday he begged some bread at a cottage door and crept into a lonely barn to eat it. It was warm in there, and after his meal he fell asleep among the hay. It was dark when he woke, and started trudging once more through the slushy road.

Two miles beyond Reigate a figure, a fragile figure, slipped out of the darkness to meet him.

'On the road, guv'nor?' said a husky voice. 'Then I'll come a bit of the way with you if you don't walk too fast. It's a bit lonesome walking this time of day.'

'But the pneumonia!' cried the tramp aghast.

'I died at Crawley this morning,' said the boy.

If She Bends, She Breaks

John Gordon

John Gordon

If She Bends, She Breaks

Ben had felt strange ever since the snow started falling. He looked out of the classroom window and saw that it had come again, sweeping across like a curtain. That was exactly what it seemed to be: a curtain. The snow had come down like a blank sheet in his mind, and he could remember nothing beyond it. He could not even remember getting up this morning or walking to school; yesterday was only a haze, and last week did not exist. And now, at this moment, he did not know whether it was morning or afternoon. He began to get to his feet, but dizziness made him sit down.

'I know it's been freezing hard.' Miss Carter's voice from the front of the class seemed distant. He wanted to tell her he felt unwell, but just for the moment he did not have the energy. She had her back to the stove as usual, and the eyes behind her glasses stared like a frightened horse's as they always did when she was in a passion. 'It's been freezing hard,' she repeated, 'but the ice is still far too dangerous, and nobody is to go anywhere near it. Do you understand?'

Tommy Drake, in the next desk to Ben, murmured something and grinned at somebody on Ben's other side. But he ignored Ben completely.

'Tommy Drake!' Miss Carter had missed nothing. 'What did you say?'

'Nothing, miss.'

'Then why are you grinning like a jackass? If there's a joke, we all want to hear it. On your feet.'

As Tommy pushed back his chair, Ben smiled at him weakly, but Tommy seemed to be in no mood for him and winked at somebody else as though Ben himself was not there.

'Well?' Miss Carter was waiting.

Tommy stood in silence.

'Very well. If you are not going to share your thoughts with the rest of us, perhaps you will remind me of what I was saying a moment ago.'

'About the ice, miss?'

'And what about the ice?'

'That it's dangerous, miss.' Then Tommy, who did not lack courage, went on, 'What I was saying was that you can always tell if it's safe.'

'Oh you can, can you?' Miss Carter pursed her lips, and again waited.

'If she cracks, she bears,' said Tommy. 'If she bends, she breaks.' It was a lesson they all knew in the flat Fenland where everybody skated in winter. A solid cracking sound in the ice was better than a soft bending. But it meant nothing to Miss Carter.

'Stuff and nonsense!' she cried.

'But everybody know it's true.' Tommy had justice on his side and his round face was getting red.

'Old wives' tales!' Miss Carter was not going to listen to reason. 'Sit down.'

Ben saw that Tommy was going to argue, and the sudden urge to back him up made him forget his dizziness. He got to his feet. 'It's quite true, miss,' he said. 'I've tried it out.'

She paid no attention to him. She glared at Tommy. 'Sit down!'

Tommy obeyed, and Miss Carter pulled her cardigan tighter over her dumpy figure.

'Listen to me, all of you.' Her voice was shrill. 'I don't care what anybody says in the village; I won't have any of you go anywhere near that ice. Do you hear? Nobody!' She paused, and then added softly, 'You all know what can happen.'

She had succeeded in silencing the classroom and, as she turned away to her own desk, she muttered something to the front row who began putting their books away. It was time for break.

Ben was still standing. In her passion she seemed not to have seen him. 'What's up with her?' he said, but Tommy was on his feet and heading towards the cloakroom with the rest.

The dizziness came over Ben again. Could nobody see that he was unwell? Or was his illness something so terrible that everybody wanted to ignore it? The classroom had emptied, and Miss Carter was wiping her nose on a crumpled paper handkerchief. He would tell her how he felt, and perhaps she would get his sister to walk home with him. He watched her head swing towards him and he opened his mouth to speak, but her glance swept over him and she turned to follow the others.

A movement outside one of the classroom's tall, narrow, windows made him look out. One boy was already in the yard, and the snow was thick and inviting. Beyond the railings there was the village and, through a gap in the houses, he could see the flat fens stretching away in a desert of whiteness. He knew it all. He had not lost his memory. The stuffiness of the classroom was to blame – and outside there was delicious coolness, and space. Without bothering to follow the others to the cloakroom for his coat, he went out.

There was still only the boy in the playground; a new kid kicking up snow. He was finding the soft patches, not already trodden, and, as he ploughed into them, he made the snow smoke around his ankles so that he almost seemed to lack feet.

Ben went across to him and said, 'They let you out early, did they?'

The new kid raised his head and looked at the others who were now crowding out through the door. 'I reckon,' he said.

'Me an' all,' said Ben. It wasn't strictly true, but he didn't mind bending the truth a bit as he had been feeling ill. But not any more. 'Where d'you come from?' he asked.

'Over yonder.' The new kid nodded vaguely beyond the railings and then went back to kicking snow. 'It's warm, ain't it?' he said, watching the powder drift around his knees. 'When you get used to it.'

'What do your dad do?'

'Horseman,' said the kid, and that was enough to tell Ben where he lived and where his father worked. Only one farm for miles had working horses. Tommy's family, the Drakes, had always had horses and were rich enough to have them working alongside tractors, as a kind of hobby.

'You live along Pingle Bank, then,' said Ben. The horseman had a cottage there near the edge of the big drainage canal, the Pingle, that cut a straight, deep channel across the flat fens.

'That's right,' said the kid, and looked up at the sky. 'More of it comin'.'

The clouds had thickened over the winter sun and, in the grey light, snow had begun to fall again. The kid held his face up to it. 'Best time o' the year, winter. Brings you out into the open, don't it?'

'Reckon,' Ben agreed. 'If them clouds was in summer we should be gettin' soaked.'

'I hate gettin' wet.' The kid's face was pale, and snow was resting on his eyelashes.

'Me an' all.'

They stood side by side and let the snow fall on them. The kid was quite right; it seemed warm.

Then the snowball fight rolled right up to them and charging through the middle of it came Tommy, pulling Ben's sister on her sledge. Just like him to have taken over the sledge and Jenny and barge into the new kid as though he was nobody. Ben stooped, rammed snow into two hard fistfuls and hurled them with all his force at Tommy's red face. He was usually a good shot but he missed, and Tommy was yelling at Jenny as she laboured to make snowballs and pile them on the sledge.

'They ain't no good! Look, they're fallin' apart.' Tommy crouched and swept them all back into the snow.

Jenny had no height but a lot of temper. She was on her feet, her face as red as his, and yanked her sledge away.

'Bring that back!' he yelled, but Ben was already charging at him.

Tommy must have been off-balance because it took no more than a touch to push him sideways and send him into the snow flat on his back.

'You want to leave my sister alone.' Ben sat on his chest with his knees on Tommy's arms. 'Tell her you're sorry.'

He and Tommy were the same size, both strong, and sometimes they banged their heads together just to see who would be the first to back off. But this time, without any effort or even bothering to answer him,

Tommy sat up and spilled Ben off his chest as though he had no weight at all. And, as he tilted back help-lessly, Ben saw the new kid standing by, watching.

'Hi!' he shouted. 'Snowball fight. You're on my side.'

The kid looked pretty useful; pale, but solid. And Ben needed help.

'You done it wrong,' the new kid said to Ben and, without hurrying, he stepped forward.

The kid reached out to where Tommy was still sitting and put a hand over his face, spreading out pale, cold fingers across his mouth and eyes. He seemed merely to stroke him, but Tommy fell backwards.

'You don't need no pressure,' said the kid. 'All you got to do is let 'em know you're there.'

'You got him!' Ben had rolled away to let the kid tackle Tommy alone. 'Show us your stuff!'

The kid seemed to be in no hurry, and Tommy lay where he was, one startled eye showing between the pal-lid fingers. Any second now and there would be a quick thrust of limbs and Tommy would send the kid flying. It was stupid to wait for it; Ben started forward to stop the massacre.

But then the kid looked up. The snow was still in his eyelashes, and a crust of it was at the corners of his mouth, like ice.

'Want me to do any more?' he asked.

In the rest of the playground, shouts of snowfights echoed against the high windows and dark walls of the old school building, but in this corner the grey clouds seemed to hang lower as if to deaden the kid's voice.

'I asked you,' he said. 'You want to see me do some more?'

Tommy stirred, gathering himself to push. In a mo-ment the boy would pay for being so careless, unless he had some trick and was pressing on a nerve. Ben wanted to see what would happen. He nodded.

The kid did not look away from Ben, but his hand left Tommy's face. And Tommy did not get up. He simply lay there with his eyes and mouth wide open. He looked scared.

The kid, still crouching, began to stroke the snow. He curved his fingers and raked it, dusting the white powder into Tommy's hair, then over his brow and his eyes; and then the kid's hand, so pale it could not be seen in the snow, was over Tommy's lips, and snow was being thrust into the gaping mouth. The kid leant over him and Tommy was terrified. He tried to shout, but more snow was driven into his mouth. He rolled over, thrashing helplessly.

The kid paused as though waiting for instructions. But Ben, curious to see what Tommy would do, waited.

It was then that the brittle little sound of a handbell reached them. It came from the porch where Miss Carter was calling them in. But suddenly the sound ceased, and even the shouting of the snowfights died. The whole playground had seen her drop the bell.

She started forward, pushing her way through the crowds, and then, caught up in her anxiety, they came with her like black snowflakes on the wind.

It was Tommy, jerking and choking on the ground, that drew them. It was no natural fooling in the snow. He was fighting to breathe. And the new kid stood over him, looking down.

'Tommy, what have you done!' Miss Carter was stooping over him, crying out at the sight of his mouth wide open and full of whiteness. 'Oh my God!'

Ben stared across her bent back at the new kid. He simply stood where he was, a sprinkle of white in the short crop of his black hair, and gazed back at him.

'Who did this to you?' Miss Carter had thrust her fingers into the snow-gape in Tommy's face, and rolled him over so that he was coughing, gasping and heaving all at once. 'How did it happen?'

But he could not answer and she helped him to his feet and began walking with him.

'Who saw it? Which of you did this?' She had snow in her fur-lined boots and her grey hair was untidy. Her little red nose was sharp with the cold and she pointed it around the ring that had gathered, sniffing out the guilty one. 'You?' Her eyes were on Ben but had passed by almost before he had shaken his head. 'What about you?' The new kid was at the back of the crowd and did not even have to answer.

Denials came from every side, and the chattering crowd followed her into school.

Ben and the kid hung back, and were alone in the porch when the door closed and shut them out. Neither had said a word, and Ben turned towards him. The kid stood quite still gazing straight ahead as though the door was the open page of a book and he was reading it. He wore a long black jacket, and a grey scarf was wound once around his neck and hung down his back. Ben noticed for the first time that the kid's black trousers were knee-length and were tucked into long, thick socks. They looked like riding breeches, and he thought the kid must help his father with the horses. But his boots were big and clumsy, not elegant like a horseman's. There was something gawky about him; he looked poor and old-fashioned.

'You done all right,' said Ben. 'Tommy ain't bad in a fight.'

The kid turned towards him. There was still un-melted snow on his cheeks, and his eyelashes were tinged with white. His dark eyes were liquid as though he was on the verge of crying, but that was false. They had no expression at all. 'He ain't as good as he reckon,' said the kid, and left it at that.

'What class you in?' Ben asked.

'Same as you.'

'Didn't notice you.'

'I were by the stove.'

'Miss Carter always keep her bum to that, that's why it don't throw out no heat,' said Ben, but the kid did not smile. He led the way inside.

They had not been missed. Miss Carter was still fussing around Tommy. She had pulled the fireguard back from the stove so that he could go to the front of the class and sit close to it. But she was still angry.

'I'm going to catch whoever did that to you, and when I do . . .' She pinched in her little mouth until it was lipless and her eyes needled around the room.

Ben had taken his usual place at the back, and suddenly he realised the new kid had wandered off. He searched, and found him. He was sitting at a desk no more than two paces from Miss Carter and Tommy. He had one arm over the desk lid, and the other resting loosely on the back of his chair. He was quite untroubled.

'Stand up, Tommy,' Miss Carter ordered. 'Now turn round and point out who did this terrible thing.'

Tommy, a hero now, was enjoying himself. He faced the class. Ben could see the pale curve of the new kid's cheek and guessed at the deep-water look of the eyes that were turned on Tommy.

'Tommy!' said Miss Carter, and obediently Tommy looked round the room. He smirked at several people but not at Ben. He ignored him as though angry with him for what had happened yet not prepared to betray him. But there was a real risk he would get his revenge on the kid. Yet again his glance went by as though the boy's desk was empty, and he said, 'Nobody done it. I just fell over, that's all.'

The girl next to Ben whispered to her friend, 'Maybe he had a fit. That looked like it with his mouth all white. Like he was foaming.'

'Be quiet!' Miss Carter had lost her patience. 'Sit down!' she ordered Tommy, and for the rest of the afternoon she was savage, even with him.

From time to time Ben looked towards the new kid, but he kept his head bowed over his work and Ben saw no more than the black bristles of his cropped hair. Nobody attempted to speak to him because whenever anybody moved, Miss Carter snapped.

The last half-hour dragged, but then, with a rattle of pencils and a banging of desk lids, the afternoon ended. The new kid wasted no time. He was out of the door ahead of everybody else, and Ben did not catch him until he was half-way across the playground.

'Where you going?' he asked.

'The Pingle.'

'We ain't supposed to. Because of the ice.'

'I live there.'

Then Ben remembered the horseman's cottage on the bank, but he said, 'Ain't you going to hang around here a bit? We got some good slides in the yard.'

'Ice is better.'

The others, charging out at the door, prevented Ben saying more. Jenny, with her sledge, was being chased by Tommy. He was himself again and was telling her, 'Your sledge will go great on the Pingle.'

'I don't want to go,' she said.

A bigger girl butted in. 'You heard what Miss Carter said, Tommy Drake. Ain't you got no sense?'

Tommy paid no attention. 'Come on, Jenny. I ain't

got time to go home and fetch me skates or else I would. I'll bring 'em tomorrow and you can have a go. Promise.'

She was tempted, but she said, 'I don't want to go there. And you know why.'

'I won't take a step on it unless it's rock hard,' said Tommy.

'I ain't going,' said Jenny.

At the school gate, the kid moved his feet impatiently on the step. It had been cleared of snow and the metal studs on his boots rattled.

Tommy had also lost his patience. 'If she cracks she bears, if she bends she breaks. Everybody know that's true, no matter what old Carter say. And I won't budge away from the bank unless it's safe.'

'No,' said Jenny.

Suddenly the kid kicked at the steps and made sparks fly from the sole of his boot, and Tommy looked up. The wind dived over the school roof in a howl and a plunge of snow, and the kid's voice merged with it as he yelled, 'Come on!'

He and Ben ran together, and Tommy grabbed at the sledge and made for the gate. Several others came with him.

Ben and the boy kept ahead of the rest as they rounded the corner into the lane. Traffic had failed to churn up the snow and had packed it hard, almost icy, so it would have been as good as anywhere for Jenny's sledge; but Ben ran with the boy between hedges humped and white, and the others followed.

They left the road just before it climbed to the bridge across the Pingle, and they stood at the top of the bank, looking down. They were the first to come here. The grass blades, slowly arching as the snow had added petal after petal through the day, supported an unbroken roof just clear of the ground. Below them, the straight, wide channel stretched away to left and right through the flat, white land. The water had become a frozen road, and the wind had swept it almost clear, piling the snow in an endless, smooth drift on the far side.

Tommy had come up alongside them. 'You could go for miles!' he shouted.

But Jenny hung back. 'I don't like it.' The air was grey and cold and it almost smothered her small voice. 'I want to go home.'

'It ain't dark yet.' His voice yelped as though it came from the lonely seagull that angled up on a frozen gust far out over the white plain. He began to move forward. 'Let's get down there.'

'She doesn't want to go.' Ben was close to him, but Tommy paid no heed. 'Nobody's going down that bank, Tommy.' Ben stepped forward, blocking his way. 'Nobody!'

Tommy came straight on. His eyes met Ben's but their expression did not change. His whole attention was focused on the ice below and his gaze seemed to go through Ben as though he was not there.

In a sudden cold anger Ben lowered his head and lunged with both arms. He thrust at Tommy's chest with all his force. His fingers touched, but in the instant of touching they lost their grip. He thrust with all his power, but it was air alone that slid along his arms and fingers, and Tommy was past and through and plunging down the bank.

The kid, watching him, said, 'You still don't do it right.'

Tommy had taken Jenny's sledge with him, and at the ice edge he turned and shouted to them up the bank. 'Come on, all of you!'

'No!' Ben stood in front of them. 'Don't go!' He opened his arms, but they came in a group straight for him. 'Stop!' They did not answer. Their eyes did not look directly at him. They pushed into him, like a crush of cattle, pretending he was not there. He clutched at one after another but the strange weakness he had felt earlier made him too flimsy to stop anything and they were beyond him and going down to join Tommy.

'I got to teach you a few things,' said the kid.

'I don't feel too good,' said Ben. 'I think I ought to go home.'

The boy gazed at him for a moment with eyes that again seemed to be rimmed with frost, and shook his head. 'There's them down there to see to,' he said.

Slowly, Ben nodded. He had to think of Jenny.

They went down together and found Tommy still on the bank. Frozen reeds stood up through the ice and there was a seepage of water at the edge that made them all hesitate. All except the new kid. He put one foot on it, testing.

'If she cracks she bears,' he said.

Ben watched. The boy had plenty of courage. He was leaning forward now, putting all his weight on the ice.

'She cracks,' he said.

But Ben had heard nothing. 'No,' he called out. 'She bends.'

He was too late. The boy had stepped out onto the ice. Then Ben heard the crack under his boots, and the echo of it ringing from bank to bank and away along the endless ice in thin winter music.

The boy moved out until he was a figure in black in the middle of the channel. 'She bears,' he called out, and Ben, who knew he could never stop the others now, stepped out to be with him.

There was no crack this time, but the ice held. He

could feel the gentle pulse of it as he walked towards the middle. There was something almost like a smile on the new kid's face. 'Both on us done it,' he said, and Ben nodded.

On the bank there was a squabble. The big girl, protecting Jenny, was trying to pull the sledge rope from Tommy. 'Let her have her sledge,' she said. 'You didn't ought to have brung her here.'

'It's safe enough.'

'I don't care whether it's safe or not, you didn't ought to have brung her. Not Jenny, of all people.'

'Why all the fuss about Jenny?' said Ben to the kid. 'I don't know what they're going on about.'

'Don't you?' The kid's eyes, darkening as the day dwindled, rested on him. Far away along the length of the frozen channel, snow and sky and darkness joined.

'Why don't they come out here?' said Ben. 'They can see us.'

'We can go and fetch 'em,' said the kid.

'How?'

'Get hold of that sledge. They'll follow.'

Ben hesitated. Perhaps he was too weak to do even that.

The kid saw his doubt, and said, 'You've pulled a sledge before, ain't you?' Ben nodded. 'Well, all you got to do is remember what it feel like. That's all.'

Ben had to rely on him. Everything he had tried himself had gone wrong. He walked across to where Tommy was still arguing.

'See what you done to her,' the girl was saying. She had her arm around Jenny's shoulder and Jenny was crying, snuffling into her gloves. 'Ain't you got no feelings, Tommy Drake?'

'Well, just because it happened once,' said Tommy, 'that ain't to say it's going to happen again.'

'Wasn't just once!' The girl thrust her head forward, accusing him. 'There was another time.' She lifted her arm from Jenny's shoulder and pointed up the bank behind her. 'There was a boy lived up there, along Pingle Bank; he came down here and went through the ice one winter time, and they never found him till it thawed.'

'That were a long time ago,' said Tommy. 'Years before any of us was born.'

'You ought to know about that if anybody do, Tommy Drake. That boy's father worked on your farm. Everybody know about that even if it was all them years ago. His father were a horseman and lived along the bank.'

'Hey!' Ben was close to Tommy. 'Just like the new kid.'

But even that did not make Tommy turn his way. Ben reached for the sledge rope and jerked it. He felt the rope in his fingers just before it slipped through and fell, but he had tugged it from Tommy's grasp and the sledge ran out on to the ice.

'Come on, Tommy,' he said. 'Come with me and the new kid.'

The girl was watching the sledge and accusing Tommy. 'What did you want to do that for?'

'I didn't,' he said.

'I did it,' said Ben, but nobody looked towards him.

The girl was furious with Tommy. 'Just look what you done. Now you'll have to leave it.'

Tommy had put one foot on the ice, testing it. 'I ain't frit,' he said. 'I reckon it'll hold.'

'Of course it will,' Ben encouraged him. 'We're both out here, ain't we?' He paused and looked over his shoulder to make sure, but the kid was still there, watching. 'Two of us. Me and him.'

Tommy had both feet on the ice and had taken

another step. 'See,' he called to the others on the bank. 'Nothing to it.'

'Don't you make a parade out there by yourself any longer, Tommy Drake.' The girl pulled Jenny's face tighter into her shoulder and made an effort to muffle Jenny's ears. She leant forward as far as she could, keeping her voice low so that Jenny should not hear. 'Can't you see what you're doing to her? This were just the place where Ben went through the ice last winter.'

Tommy, stamping to make the ice ring beneath him, kept·his back to her. 'If she cracks,' he said, 'she bears. If she bends, she breaks.'

'Can't you hear?' said the girl. 'This is just the place where Ben were drowned!'

The snow came in a sudden flurry, putting a streaked curtain between Ben and the rest of them. It was then that he remembered. He remembered everything. The kid had come up to stand beside him, and they stood together and watched.

The ice under Tommy sagged as they knew it would. They heard the soft rending as it split, and they saw its broken edge rear up. They heard the yell and the slither, and remembered the cold gulp of the black water that, with years between, had swallowed each of them. But now it was somebody else who slid under.

Then Jenny's scream reached Ben through the wind that was pushing down the channel as the night came on. She should be at home; not out here watching this. He stooped to the sledge and pushed.

On the bank they saw nothing but a tight spiral of snow whipped up from the ice, but the sledge slid into the water beside Tommy and floated. He grabbed at it.

From out on the ice they saw the girl, held by the others, reach from the bank and grasp the rope, and then Tommy, soaking and freezing, crawled into the white snow and made it black. They watched as the whole group, sobbing and murmuring, climbed the bank, showed for a few moments against the darkening sky and were gone.

In the empty channel the two figures stood motionless. Their eyes gazed unblinking through the swirl as the snow came again, hissing as it blew between the frozen reeds.

The July Ghost

A S Byatt

A S Byatt

The July Ghost

'I think I must move out of where I'm living,' he said.
'I have this problem with my landlady.'

He picked a long, bright hair off the back of her dress,
so deftly that the act seemed simply considerate. He had
been skilful at balancing glass, plate and cutlery, too.
He had a look of dignified misery, like a dejected hawk.
She was interested.

'What sort of problem? Amatory,[1] financial, or
domestic?'

'None of those, really. Well, not financial.'

He turned the hair on his finger, examining it intently, not meeting her eye.

'Not financial. Can you tell me? I might know somewhere you could stay. I know a lot of people.'

'You would.' He smiled shyly. 'It's not an easy problem to describe. There's just the two of us. I occupy
the attics. Mostly.'

He came to a stop. He was obviously reserved and
secretive. But he was telling her something. This is
usually attractive.

'Mostly?' Encouraging him.

'Oh, it's not like *that*. Well, not . . . Shall we sit
down?'

They moved across the party, which was a big party,

[1] to do with love life

50

on a hot day. He stopped and found a bottle and filled
her glass. He had not needed to ask what she was drinking. They sat side by side on a sofa: he admired the
brilliant poppies bold on her emerald dress, and her
pretty sandals. She had come to London for the summer
to work in the British Museum. She could really have
managed with microfilm in Tucson for what little
manuscript research was needed, but there was a dragging love affair to end. There is an age at which,
however desperately happy one is in stolen moments,
days, or weekends with one's married professor, one
either prises him loose or cuts and runs. She had had
a stab at both, and now considered she had successfully
cut and run. So it was nice to be immediately ap-
preciated. Problems are capable of solution. She said as
much to him, turning her soft face to his ravaged one,
swinging the long bright hair. It had begun a year ago,
he told her in a rush, at another party actually; he had
met this woman, the landlady in question, and had
made, not immediately, a kind of *faux pas*,[1] he now saw,
and she had been very decent, all things considered,
and so . . .

He had said, 'I think I must move out of where I'm
living.' He had been quite wild, had nearly not come
to the party, but could not go on drinking alone. The
woman had considered him coolly and asked, 'Why?'
One could not, he said, go on in a place where one had
once been blissfully happy, and was now miserable,
however convenient the place. Convenient, that was, for
work, and friends, and things that seemed, as he mentioned them, ashy and insubstantial compared to the
memory and the hope of opening the door and finding
Anne outside it, laughing and breathless, waiting to be

___

embarrassing remark

told what he had read, or thought, or eaten, or felt that day. Someone I loved left, he told the woman. Reticent on that occasion too, he bit back the flurry of sentences about the total unexpectedness of it, the arriving back and finding only an envelope on a clean table, and spaces in the bookshelves, the record stack, the kitchen cupboard. It must have been planned for weeks, she must have been thinking it out while he rolled on her, while she poured wine for him, while ... No, no. Vituperation is undignified and in this case what he felt was lower and worse than rage: just pure, child-like loss. 'One ought not to mind places,' he said to the woman. 'But one does,' she had said. 'I know.'

She had suggested to him that he could come and be her lodger, then; she had, she said, a lot of spare space going to waste, and her husband wasn't there much. 'We've not had a lot to say to each other, lately.' He could be quite self-contained, there was a kitchen and a bathroom in the attics; she wouldn't bother him. There was a large garden. It was possibly this that decided him: it was very hot, central London, the time of year when a man feels he would give anything to live in a room opening on to grass and trees, not a high flat in a dusty street. And if Anne came back, the door would be locked and mortice-locked. He could stop thinking about Anne coming back. That was a decisive move: Anne thought he wasn't decisive. He would live without Anne.

For some weeks after he moved in he had seen very little of the woman. They met on the stairs, and once she came up, on a hot Sunday, to tell him he must feel free to use the garden. He had offered to do some weeding and mowing and she had accepted. That was the weekend her husband came back, driving furiously up to the front door, running in, and calling in the empty hall, 'Imogen, Imogen!' To which she had replied, uncharacteristically, by screaming hysterically. There was nothing in her husband, Noel's, appearance to warrant this reaction; their lodger, peering over the banister at the sound, had seen their upturned faces in the stairwell and watched hers settle into its usual prim and placid expression as he did so. Seeing Noel, a balding, fluffytempled, stooping thirty-five or so, shabby corduroy suit, cotton polo neck, he realised he was now able to guess her age, as he had not been. She was a very neat woman, faded blonde, her hair in a knot on the back of her head, her legs long and slender, her eyes downcast. Mild was not quite the right word for her, though. She explained then that she had screamed because Noel had come home unexpectedly and startled her: she was sorry. It seemed a reasonable explanation. The extraordinary vehemence of the screaming was probably an echo in the stairwell. Noel seemed wholly downcast by it, all the same.

He had kept out of the way, that weekend, taking the stairs two at a time and lightly, feeling a little aggrieved, looking out of his kitchen window into the lovely, over-grown garden, that they were lurking indoors, wasting all the summer sun. At Sunday lunch-time he had heard the husband, Noel, shouting on the stairs.

'I can't go on, if you go on like that. I've done my best, I've tried to get through. Nothing will shift you, will it, you won't *try*, will you, you just go on and on. Well, I have my life to live, you can't throw a life away . . . can you?'

He had crept out again on to the dark upper landing and seen her standing, half-way down the stairs, quite still, watching Noel wave his arms and roar, or almost roar, with a look of impassive patience, as though this nuisance must pass off. Noel swallowed and gasped; he turned his face up to her and said plaintively, 'You do see I can't stand it? I'll be in touch, shall I? You must want . . . you must need . . . you must . . .'

She didn't speak.

'If you need anything, you know where to get me.'

'Yes.'

'Oh, well . . .' said Noel, and went to the door. She watched him, from the stairs, until it was shut, and then came up again, step by step, as though it was an effort, a little, and went on coming, past her bedroom, to his landing, to come in and ask him, entirely naturally, please to use the garden if he wanted to, and please not to mind marital rows. She was sure he understood . . . things were difficult . . . Noel wouldn't be back for some time. He was a journalist: his work took him away a lot. Just as well. She committed herself to that 'just as well'. She was a very economical speaker.

So he took to sitting in the garden. It was a lovely place: a huge, hidden, walled south London garden, with old fruit trees at the end, a wildly waving disorderly buddleia, curving beds full of old roses, and a lawn of overgrown, dense rye-grass. Over the wall at the foot was the Common, with a footpath running behind all the gardens. She came out to the shed and helped him to assemble and oil the lawnmower, standing on the little path under the apple branches while he cut an experimental serpentine across her hay. Over the wall came the high sound of children's voices, and the thunk and thud of a football. He asked her how to raise the blades: he was not mechanically minded.

'The children get quite noisy,' she said. 'And dogs. I hope they don't bother you. There aren't many safe places for children, round here.'

He replied truthfully that he never heard sounds that didn't concern him, when he was concentrating. When he'd got the lawn into shape, he was going to sit on it and do a lot of reading, try to get his mind in trim again, to write a paper on Hardy's poems, on their curiously archaic vocabulary.

'It isn't very far to the road on the other side, really,' she said. 'It just seems to be. The Common is an illusion of space, really. Just a spur of brambles and gorse-bushes and bits of football pitch between two fast four-laned main roads. I hate London commons.'

'There's a lovely smell, though, from the gorse and the wet grass. It's a pleasant illusion.'

'No illusions are pleasant,' she said, decisively, and went in. He wondered what she did with her time: apart from little shopping expeditions she seemed to be always in the house. He was sure that when he'd met her she'd been introduced as having some profession: vaguely literary, vaguely academic, like everyone he knew. Perhaps she wrote poetry in her north-facing living-room. He had no idea what it would be like. Women generally wrote emotional poetry, much nicer than men, as Kingsley Amis[1] has stated, but she seemed, despite her placid stillness, too spare and too fierce – grim? – for that. He remembered the screaming. Perhaps she wrote Plath-like[2] chants of violence. He didn't think that quite fitted the bill, either. Perhaps she was a freelance radio journalist. He didn't bother to ask anyone who might

---

[1] a contemporary novelist, poet and critic

[2] Sylvia Plath was an intense American poet who committed suicide in 1963. She was married to the poet Ted Hughes.

be a common acquaintance. During the whole year, he explained to the American at the party, he hadn't actually *discussed* her with anyone. Of course he wouldn't, she agreed vaguely and warmly. She knew he wouldn't. He didn't see why he shouldn't, in fact, but went on, for the time, with his narrative.

They had got to know each other a little better over the next few weeks, at least on the level of borrowing tea, or even sharing pots of it. The weather had got hotter. He had found an old-fashioned deck-chair, with faded striped canvas, in the shed, and had brushed it over and brought it out on to his mown lawn, where he sat writing a little, reading a little, getting up and pulling up a tuft of couch grass. He had been wrong about the children not bothering him: there was a succession of incursions by all sizes of children looking for all sizes of balls, which bounced to his feet, or crashed in the shrubs, or vanished in the herbaceous border, black and white footballs, beach-balls with concentric circles of primary colours, acid yellow tennis balls. The children came over the wall: black faces, brown faces, floppy long hair, shaven heads, respectable dotted sun-hats and camouflaged cotton army hats from Milletts. They came over easily, as though they were used to it, sandals, training shoes, a few bare toes, grubby sunburned legs, cotton skirts, jeans, football shorts. Sometimes, perched on the top, they saw him and gestured at the balls; one or two asked permission. Sometimes he threw a ball back, but was apt to knock down a few knobby little unripe apples or pears. There was a gate in the wall, under the fringing trees, which he once tried to open, spending time on rusty bolts only to discover that the lock was new and secure, and the key not in it.

The boy sitting in the tree did not seem to be looking

for a ball. He was in a fork of the tree nearest the gate, swinging his legs, doing something to a knot in a frayed end of rope that was attached to the branch he sat on. He wore blue jeans and training shoes, and a brilliant tee shirt, striped in the colours of the spectrum, arranged in the right order, which the man on the grass found visually pleasing. He had rather long blond hair, falling over his eyes, so that his face was obscured.

'Hey, you. Do you think you ought to be up there? It might not be safe.'

The boy looked up, grinned, and vanished monkey-like over the wall. He had a nice, frank grin, friendly, not cheeky.

He was there again, the next day, leaning back in the crook of the tree, arms crossed. He had on the same shirt and jeans. The man watched him, expecting him to move again, but he sat, immobile, smiling down pleasantly, and then staring up at the sky. The man read a little, looked up, saw him still there, and said, 'Have you lost anything?'

The child did not reply: after a moment he climbed down a little, swung along the branch hand over hand, dropped to the ground, raised an arm in salute, and was up over the usual route over the wall.

Two days later he was lying on his stomach on the edge of the lawn, out of the shade, this time in a white tee shirt with a pattern of blue ships and water-lines on it, his bare feet and legs stretched in the sun. He was chewing a grass stem, and studying the earth, as though watching for insects. The man said, 'Hi, there,' and the boy looked up, met his look with intensely blue eyes under long lashes, smiled with the same complete warmth and openness, and returned his look to the earth.

He felt reluctant to inform on the boy, who seemed

so harmless and considerate: but when he met him walking out of the kitchen door, spoke to him, and got no answer but the gentle smile before the boy ran off towards the wall, he wondered if he should speak to his landlady. So he asked her, did she mind the children coming in the garden. She said no, children must look for balls, that was part of being children. He persisted – they sat there, too, and he had met one coming out of the house. He hadn't seemed to be doing any harm, the boy, but you couldn't tell. He thought she should know.

He was probably a friend of her son's, she said. She looked at him kindly and explained. Her son had run off the Common with some other children, two years ago, in the summer, in July, and had been killed on the road. More or less instantly, she had added drily, as though calculating that just *enough* information would preclude the need for further questions. He said he was sorry, very sorry, feeling to blame, which was ridiculous, and a little injured, because he had not known about her son, and might inadvertently have made a fool of himself with some casual reference whose ignorance would be embarrassing.

What was the boy like, she said. The one in the house? 'I don't – talk to his friends. I find it painful. It could be Timmy, or Martin. They might have lost something, or want . . .'

He described the boy. Blond, about ten at a guess, he was not very good at children's ages, very blue eyes, slightly built, with a rainbow-striped tee shirt and blue jeans, mostly though not always – oh, and those football practice shoes, black and green. And the other tee shirt, with the ships and wavy lines. And an extraordinarily nice smile. A really *warm* smile. A nice-looking boy.

He was used to her being silent. But this silence went

on and on and on. She was just staring into the garden. After a time, she said, in her precise conversational tone, 'The only thing I want, the only thing I want at all in this world, is to see that boy.'

She stared at the garden and he stared with her, until the grass began to dance with empty light, and the edges of the shrubbery wavered. For a brief moment he shared the strain of not seeing the boy. Then she gave a little sigh, sat down, neatly as always, and passed out at his feet.

After this she became, for her, voluble. He didn't move her after she fainted, but sat patiently by her, until she stirred and sat up; then he fetched her some water, and would have gone away, but she talked.

'I'm too rational to see ghosts, I'm not someone who would see anything there was to see, I don't believe in an after-life, I don't see how anyone can, I always found a kind of satisfaction for myself in the idea that one just came to an end, to a sliced-off stop. But that was myself; I didn't think *he* – not *he* – I thought ghosts were – what people *wanted* to see, or were afraid to see . . . and after he died, the best hope I had, it sounds silly, was that I would go mad enough so that instead of waiting every day for him to come home from school and rattle the letter-box I might actually have the illusion of seeing or hearing him come in. Because I can't stop my body and mind waiting, every day, I can't let go. And his bedroom, sometimes at night I go in, I think I might just for a moment forget he *wasn't* in there sleeping, I think I would pay almost anything – anything at all – for a moment of seeing him like I used to. In his pyjamas, with his – his – his hair . . . ruffled, and, his . . . you said, his . . . that *smile*.

'When it happened, they got Noel, and Noel came in and shouted my name, like he did the other day, that's why I screamed, because it – seemed the same – and then they said, he is dead, and I thought coolly, *is* dead, that will go on and on and on till the end of time, it's a continuous present tense, one thinks the most ridiculous things, there I was thinking about grammar, the verb to be, when it ends to be dead . . . And then I came out into the garden, and I half saw, in my mind's eye, a kind of ghost of his face, just the eyes and hair, coming towards me – like every day waiting for him to come home, the way you think of your son, with such pleasure, when he's – not there – and I – I thought – no, I won't *see* him, because he is dead, and I won't dream about him because he is dead, I'll be rational and practical and continue to live because one must, and there was Noel . . .

'I got it wrong, you see, I was so *sensible*, and then I was so shocked because I couldn't get to want anything – I couldn't *talk* to Noel – I – I – made Noel take away, destroy, all the photos, I – didn't dream, you can will not to dream, I didn't . . . visit a grave, flowers, there isn't any point. I was so sensible. Only my body wouldn't stop waiting and all it wants is to – to see that boy. *That* boy. That boy you – saw.'

He did not say that he might have seen another boy, maybe even a boy who had been given the tee shirts and jeans afterwards. He did not say, though the idea crossed his mind, that maybe what he had seen was some kind of impression from her terrible desire to see a boy where nothing was. The boy had had nothing terrible, no aura of pain about him: he had been, his memory insisted, such a pleasant, courteous, self-contained boy, with his own purposes. And in fact the woman herself almost immediately raised the possibility that what he had seen was what she desired to see, a kind of mix-up of radio waves, like when you overheard police messages on the radio, or got BBC 1 on a switch that said ITV. She was thinking fast, and went on almost immediately to say that perhaps his sense of loss, his loss of Anne, which was what had led her to feel she could bear his presence in her house, was what had brought them – dare she say – near enough, for their wavelengths to mingle, perhaps, had made him susceptible . . . You mean, he had said, we are a kind of emotional vacuum, between us, that must be filled. Something like that, she had said, and had added, 'But I don't believe in ghosts.'

Anne, he thought, could not be a ghost, because she was elsewhere, with someone else, doing for someone else those little things she had done so gaily for him, tasty little suppers, bits of research, a sudden vase of unusual flowers, a new bold shirt, unlike his own cautious taste, but suiting him, suiting him. In a sense, Anne was worse lost because voluntarily absent, an absence that could not be loved because love was at an end, for Anne.

'I don't suppose you will, now,' the woman was saying. 'I think talking would probably stop any – mixing of messages, if that's what it is, don't you? But – if – *if* he comes again' – and here for the first time her eyes were full of tears – 'if – you must promise, you will *tell* me, you must promise.'

He had promised, easily enough, because he was fairly sure she was right, the boy would not be seen again. But the next day he was on the lawn, nearer than ever, sitting on the grass beside the deck-chair, his arms clasping his bent, warm brown knees, the thick, pale hair glittering in the sun. He was wearing a football shirt, this time, Chelsea's colours. Sitting down in the deck-chair, the man could have put out a hand and touched him, but did not: it was not, it seemed, a possible gesture to make. But the boy looked up and smiled, with a pleasant complicity, as though they now understood each other very well. The man tried speech: he said, 'It's nice to see you again,' and the boy nodded acknowledgement of this remark, without speaking himself. This was the beginning of communication between them, or what the man supposed to be communication. He did not think of fetching the woman. He became aware that he was in some strange way *enjoying the boy's company*. His pleasant stillness – and he sat there all morning, occasionally lying back on the grass, occasionally staring thoughtfully at the house – was calming and comfortable. The man did quite a lot of work – wrote about three reasonable pages on Hardy's original air-blue gown – and looked up now and then to make sure the boy was still there and happy.

He went to report to the woman – as he had after all promised to do – that evening. She had obviously been waiting and hoping – her unnatural calm had given way to agitated pacing, and her eyes were dark and deeper in. At this point in the story he found in himself a necessity to bowdlerise[1] for the sympathetic American, as he had indeed already begun to do. He had mentioned only a child who had 'seemed like' the woman's lost son, and he now ceased to mention the child at all, as an actor in the story, with the result that what the American woman heard was a tale of how he, the man, had become increasingly involved in the woman's solitary grief, how their two losses had become a kind

---

[1] expurgate, cut out parts which might raise a blush. Dr Bowdler (1754–1825) was an editor of Shakespeare's works who cut out anything in the plays that he thought obscene.

of *folie à deux*[1] from which he could not extricate himself. What follows is not what he told the American girl, though it may be clear at which points the bowdlerised version coincided with what he really believed to have happened. There was a sense he could not at first analyse that it was improper to talk about the boy – not because he might not be believed; that did not come into it; but because something dreadful might happen.

'He sat on the lawn all morning. In a football shirt.'

'Chelsea?'

'Chelsea.'

'What did he do? Does he look happy? Did he speak?' Her desire to know was terrible.

'He doesn't speak. He didn't move much. He seemed – very calm. He stayed a long time.'

'This is terrible. This is ludicrous. There *is no boy*.'

'No. But I saw him.'

'Why you?'

'I don't know.' A pause. 'I do *like* him.'

'He is – was – a most likeable boy.'

Some days later he saw the boy running along the landing in the evening, wearing what might have been pyjamas, in peacock towelling, or might have been a track suit. Pyjamas, the woman stated confidently, when he told her: his new pyjamas. With white ribbed cuffs, weren't they? and a white polo neck? He corroborated this, watching her cry – she cried more easily now – finding her anxiety and disturbance very hard to bear. But it never occurred to him that it was possible to break his promise to tell her when he saw the boy.

---

[1] a form of mental illness in which two people share the same delusion

That was another curious imperative from some un-defined authority.

They discussed clothes. If there were ghosts, how could they appear in clothes long burned, or rotted, or worn away by other people? You could imagine, they agreed, that something of a person might linger – as the Tibetans and others believe the soul lingers near the body before setting out on its long journey. But clothes? And in this case so many clothes? I must be seeing your memories, he told her, and she nodded fiercely, com-pressing her lips, agreeing that this was likely, adding, 'I am too rational to go mad, so I seem to be putting it on you.'

He tried a joke. 'That isn't very kind to me, to imply that madness comes more easily to me.'

'No, sensitivity. I am insensible. I was always a bit like that, and this made it worse, I am the *last* person to see any ghost that was trying to haunt me.'

'We agreed it was your memories I saw.'

'Yes. We agreed. That's rational. As rational as we can be, considering.'

All the same, the brilliance of the boy's blue regard, his gravely smiling salutation in the garden next morning, did not seem like anyone's tortured memories of earlier happiness. The man spoke to him directly then:

'Is there anything I can *do* for you? Anything you want? Can I help you?'

The boy seemed to puzzle about this for a while, in-clining his head as though hearing was difficult. Then he nodded, quickly and perhaps urgently, turned, and ran into the house, looking back to make sure he was followed. The man entered the living-room through the french windows, behind the running boy, who stopped for a moment in the centre of the room, with the man blinking behind him at the sudden transition from sun-light to comparative dark. The woman was sitting in an armchair, looking at nothing there. She often sat like that. She looked up, across the boy, at the man; and the boy, his face for the first time anxious, met the man's eyes again, asking, before he went out into the house.

'What is it? What is it? Have you seen him again? Why are you . . .?'

'He came in here. He went – out through the door.'

'I didn't see him.'

'No.'

'Did he – oh, this is so *silly* – did he see me?'

He could not remember. He told the only truth he knew.

'He brought me in here.'

'Oh, what can I do, what am I going to *do*? If I killed myself – I have thought of that – but the idea that I should be with him is an illusion I . . . this silly situation is the nearest I shall ever get. To him. He was *in here with me?*'

'Yes.'

And she was crying again. Out in the garden he could see the boy, swinging agile on the apple branch.

He was not quite sure, looking back, when he had thought he had realised what the boy had wanted him to do. This was also, at the party, his worst piece of what he called bowdlerisation, though in some sense it was clearly the opposite of bowdlerisation. He told the American girl that he had come to the conclusion that it was the woman herself who had wanted it, though there was in fact, throughout, no sign of her wanting anything except to see the boy, as she said. The boy, bolder and more frequent, had appeared several nights running on the landing, wandering in and out of bathrooms and bedrooms, restlessly, a little agitated, questing almost, until it had 'come to' the man that what he required was to be re-engendered,[1] for him, the man, to give to his mother another child, into which he could peacefully vanish. The idea was so clear that it was like another imperative, though he did not have the courage to ask the child to confirm it. Possibly this was out of delicacy – the child was too young to be talked to about sex. Possibly there were other reasons. Possibly he was mistaken: the situation was making him hysterical, he felt action of some kind was required and must be possible. He could not spend the rest of the summer, the rest of his life, describing non-existent tee shirts and blond smiles.

He could think of no sensible way of embarking on his venture, so in the end simply walked into her bedroom one night. She was lying there, reading; when she saw him her instinctive gesture was to hide, not her bare arms and throat, but her book. She seemed, in fact, quite unsurprised to see his pyjamaed figure, and, after she had recovered her coolness, brought out the book definitely and laid it on the bedspread.

'My new taste in illegitimate literature. I keep them in a box under the bed.'

Ena Twigg, Medium. The Infinite Hive. The Spirit World. Is There Life After Death?

'Pathetic,' she proffered.

He sat down delicately on the bed.

'Please, don't grieve so. Please, let yourself be comforted. Please . . .'

[1] re-conceived and born again

He put an arm round her. She shuddered. He pulled her closer. He asked why she had had only the one son, and she seemed to understand the purport of his question, for she tried, angular and chilly, to lean on him a little, she became apparently compliant. 'No real reason,' she assured him, no material reason. Just her husband's profession and lack of inclination: that covered it.

'Perhaps,' he suggested, 'if she would be comforted a little, perhaps she could hope, perhaps . . .'

For comfort then, she said, dolefully, and lay back, pushing Ena Twigg off the bed with one fierce gesture, then lying placidly. He got in beside her, put his arms round her, kissed her cold cheek, thought of Anne, of what was never to be again. Come on, he said to the woman, you must live, you must try to live, let us hold each other for comfort.

She hissed at him 'Don't *talk*' between clenched teeth, so he stroked her lightly, over her nightdress, breasts and buttocks and long stiff legs, composed like an effigy on an Elizabethan tomb. She allowed this, trembling slightly, and then trembling violently: he took this to be a sign of some mixture of pleasure and pain, of the return of life to stone. He put a hand between her legs and she moved them heavily apart; he heaved himself over her and pushed, unsuccessfully. She was contorted and locked tight: frigid, he thought grimly, was not the word. *Rigor mortis*, his mind said to him, before she began to scream.

He was ridiculously cross about this. He jumped away and said quite rudely, 'Shut up,' and then ungraciously, 'I'm sorry.' She stopped screaming as suddenly as she had begun and made one of her painstaking economical explanations.

'Sex and death don't go. I can't afford to let go of

my grip on myself. I hoped. What you hoped. It was a bad idea. I apologise.'

'Oh, never mind,' he said and rushed out again on to the landing, feeling foolish and almost in tears for warm, lovely Anne.

The child was on the landing, waiting. When the man saw him, he looked questioning, and then turned his face against the wall and leant there, rigid, his shoulders hunched, his hair hiding his expression. There was a similarity between woman and child. The man felt, for the first time, almost uncharitable towards the boy, and then felt something else.

'Look, I'm sorry. I tried. I did try. Please turn round.'

Uncompromising, rigid, clenched back view.

'Oh well,' said the man, and went into his bedroom.

So now, he said to the American woman at the party, I feel a fool, I feel embarrassed, I feel we are hurting, not helping each other, I feel it isn't a refuge. Of course you feel that, she said, of course you're right – it was temporarily necessary, it helped both of you, but you've got to live your life. Yes, he said, I've done my best, I've tried to get through, I have my life to live. Look, she said, I want to help, I really do, I have these wonderful friends I'm renting this flat from, why don't you come, just for a few days, just for a break, why don't you? They're real sympathetic people, you'd like them, I like them, you could get your emotions kind of straightened out. She'd probably be glad to see the back of you, she must feel as bad as you do, she's got to relate to her situation in her own way in the end. We all have.

He said he would think about it. He knew he had

elected to tell the sympathetic American because he had sensed she would be – would offer – a way out. He had to get out. He took her home from the party and went back to his house and landlady without seeing her into her flat. They both knew that this reticence was promising – that he hadn't come in then, because he meant to come later. Her warmth and readiness were like sunshine, she was open. He did not know what to say to the woman.

In fact, she made it easy for him: she asked, briskly, if he now found it perhaps uncomfortable to stay, and he replied that he had felt he should move on, he was of so little use . . . Very well, she had agreed, and had added crisply that it had to be better for everyone if 'all this' came to an end. He remembered the firmness with which she had told him that no illusions were pleasant. She was strong: too strong for her own good. It would take years to wear away that stony, closed, simply sur-viving insensibility. It was not his job. He would go. All the same, he felt bad.

He got out his suitcases and put some things in them. He went down to the garden, nervously, and put away the deck-chair. The garden was empty. There was no voices over the wall. The silence was thick and deaden-ing. He wondered, knowing he would not see the boy again, if anyone else would do so, or if, now he was gone, no one would describe a tee shirt, a sandal, a smile, seen, remembered, or desired. He went slowly up to his room again.

The boy was sitting on his suitcase, arms crossed, face frowning and serious. He held the man's look for a long moment, and then the man went and sat on his bed.

The boy continued to sit. The man found himself speaking.

'You do see I have to go? I've tried to get through. I can't get through. I'm no use to you, am I?'

The boy remained immobile, his head on one side, considering. The man stood up and walked towards him.

'Please. Let me go. What are we, in this house? A man and a woman and a child, and none of us can get through. You can't want that?'

He went as close as he dared. He had, he thought, the intention of putting his hand on or through the child. But could not bring himself to feel there was no boy. So he stood, and repeated, 'I can't get through. Do you want me to stay?'

Upon which, as he stood helplessly there, the boy turned on him again the brilliant, open, confiding, beautiful desired smile.

The Red Room

H G Wells

H G Wells

The Red Room

'I can assure you,' said I, 'that it will take a very tangible ghost to frighten me.' And I stood up before the fire with my glass in my hand.

'It is your own choosing,' said the man with the withered arm, and glanced at me askance.

'Eight-and-twenty years,' said I, 'I have lived, and never a ghost have I seen as yet.'

The old woman sat staring hard into the fire, her pale eyes wide open. 'Ah,' she broke in: 'and eight-and-twenty years you have lived and never seen the likes of this house, I reckon. There's a many things to see, when one's still but eight-and-twenty.' She swayed her head slowly from side to side. 'A many things to see and sorrow for.'

I half suspected the old people were trying to enhance the spiritual terrors of their house by their droning insistence. I put down my empty glass on the table and looked about the room, and caught a glimpse of myself, abbreviated and broadened to an impossible sturdiness, in the queer old mirror at the end of the room. 'Well,' I said, 'if I see anything tonight, I shall be so much the wiser. For I come to the business with an open mind.'

'It's your own choosing,' said the man with the withered arm once more.

I heard the sound of a stick and a shambling step on the flags in the passage outside, and the door creaked on its hinges as a second old man entered, more bent, more wrinkled, more aged even than the first. He supported himself by a single crutch, his eyes were covered by a shade, and his lower lip, half averted, hung pale and pink from his decaying yellow teeth. He made straight for an armchair on the opposite side of the table, sat down clumsily, and began to cough. The man with the withered arm gave this newcomer a short glance of positive dislike; the old woman took no notice of his arrival, but remained with her eyes fixed steadily on the fire.

'I said − it's your own choosing,' said the man with the withered arm, when the coughing had ceased for a while.

'It's my own choosing,' I answered.

The man with the shade became aware of my presence for the first time, and threw his head back for a moment and sideways, to see me. I caught a momentary glimpse of his eyes, small and bright and inflamed. Then he began to cough and splutter again.

'Why don't you drink?' said the man with the withered arm, pushing the beer towards him. The man with the shade poured out a glassful with a shaky arm that splashed half as much again on the deal table. A monstrous shadow of him crouched upon the wall and mocked his action as he poured and drank. I must confess I had scarce expected these grotesque custodians. There is to my mind something inhuman in senility, something crouching and atavistic;[1] the human qualities seem to drop from old people insensibly day by day. The three of them made me feel uncomfortable, with their gaunt silences, their bent carriage, their evident unfriendliness to me and to one another.

[1] primitive

'If,' said I, 'you will show me to this haunted room of yours, I will make myself comfortable there.'

The old man with the cough jerked his head back so suddenly that it startled me, and shot another glance of his red eyes at me from under the shade; but no one answered me. I waited a minute, glancing from one to the other.

'If,' I said a little louder, 'if you will show me to this haunted room of yours, I will relieve you from the task of entertaining me.'

'There's a candle on the slab outside the door,' said the man with the withered arm, looking at my feet as he addressed me. 'But if you go to the red room to-night — '.

('This night of all nights!' said the old woman.)

'You go alone.'

'Very well,' I answered. 'And which way do I go?'

'You go along the passage for a bit,' said he, 'until you come to a door, and through that is a spiral stair-case, and half-way up that is a landing and another door covered with baize. Go through that and down the long corridor to the end, and the red room is on your left up the steps.'

'Have I got that right?' I said, and repeated his directions. He corrected me in one particular.

'And are you really going?' said the man with the shade, looking at me again for the third time, with that queer, unnatural tilting of the face.

('This night of all nights!' said the old woman.)

'It is what I came for,' I said, and moved towards the door. As I did so, the old man with the shade rose and staggered round the table, so as to be closer to the others and to the fire. At the door I turned and looked at them, and saw they were all close together, dark against the firelight, staring at me over their shoulders, with an intent expression on their ancient faces.

'Good night,' I said, setting the door open.

'It's your own choosing,' said the man with the withered arm.

I left the door wide open until the candle was well alight, and then I shut them in and walked down the chilly, echoing passage.

I must confess that the oddness of these three old pensioners in whose charge her ladyship had left the castle, and the deep-toned, old-fashioned furniture of the housekeeper's room in which they forgathered, affected me in spite of my efforts to keep myself at a matter of fact phase. They seemed to belong to another age, an older age, an age when things spiritual were different from this of ours, less certain; an age when omens and witches were credible, and ghosts beyond denying. Their very existence was spectral; the cut of their clothing, fashions born in dead brains. The ornaments and conveniences of the room about them were ghostly – the thoughts of vanished men, which still haunted rather than participated in the world of today. But with an effort I sent such thoughts to the right-about. The long, draughty subterranean passage was chilly and dusty, and my candle flared and made the shadows cower and quiver. The echoes rang up and down the spiral staircase, and a shadow came sweeping up after me, and one fled before me into the darkness overhead. I came to the landing and stopped there for a moment, listening to a rustling that I fancied I heard; then, satisfied of the absolute silence, I pushed open the baize-covered door and stood in the corridor.

The effect was scarcely what I expected, for the moonlight coming in by the great window on the grand staircase picked out everything in vivid black shadow or silvery illumination. Everything was in its place; the house might have been deserted on the yesterday instead of eighteen months ago. There were candles in the sockets of the sconces,[1] and whatever dust had gathered on the carpets or upon the polished flooring was distributed so evenly as to be invisible in the moonlight. I was about to advance, and stopped abruptly. A bronze group stood upon the landing, hidden from me by the corner of the wall, but its shadow fell with marvellous distinctness upon the white panelling and gave me the impression of some one crouching to waylay me. I stood rigid for half a minute perhaps. Then, with my hand in the pocket that held my revolver, I advanced, only to discover a Ganymede[2] and Eagle glistening in the moonlight. That incident for a time restored my nerve, and a porcelain Chinaman on a buhl table,[3] whose head rocked silently as I passed him, scarcely startled me.

The door to the red room and the steps up to it were in a shadowy corner. I moved my candle from side to side, in order to see clearly the nature of the recess in which I stood before opening the door. Here it was, thought I, that my predecessor was found, and the memory of that story gave me a sudden twinge of apprehension. I glanced over my shoulder at the Ganymede in the moonlight, and opened the door of the red room rather hastily, with my face half-turned to the pallid silence of the landing.

I entered, closed the door behind me at once, turned the key I found in the lock within, and stood with the candle held aloft, surveying the scene of my vigil, the great red room of Lorraine Castle, in which the young

---

[1] candle-brackets
[2] a cherub: Zeus' page-boy in Greek legend
[3] table inlaid with metal and precious stones

duke had died. Or, rather, in which he had begun his dying, for he had opened the door and fallen headlong down the steps I had just ascended. That had been the end of his vigil, of his gallant attempt to conquer the ghostly tradition of the place, and never, I thought, had apoplexy[1] better served the ends of superstition. And there were other and older stories that clung to the room, back to the half-credible beginning of it all, the tale of a timid wife and the tragic end that came to her husband's jest of frightening her. And looking around that large sombre room, with its shadowy window bays, its recesses and alcoves, one could well understand the legends that had sprouted in its black corners, its germinating darkness. My candle was a little tongue of light in its vastness, that failed to pierce the opposite end of the room, and left an ocean of mystery and suggestion beyond its island of light.

I resolved to make a systematic examination of the place at once, and dispel the fanciful suggestions of its obscurity before they obtained a hold upon me. After satisfying myself of the fastening of the door, I began to walk about the room, peering round each article of furniture, tucking up the valances of the bed, and opening its curtains wide. I pulled up the blinds and examined the fastenings of the several windows before closing the shutters, leant forward and looked up the blackness of the wide chimney, and tapped the dark oak panelling for any secret opening. There were two big mirrors in the room, each with a pair of sconces bearing candles, and on the mantelshelf, too, were more candles in china candlesticks. All these I lit one after the other. The fire was laid, an unexpected consideration from the old housekeeper – and I lit it, to keep down any disposition

[1] a sudden fit

to shiver, and when it was burning well, I stood round with my back to it and regarded the room again. I had pulled up a chintz-covered armchair and a table, to form a kind of barricade before me, and on this lay my revolver ready to hand. My precise examination had done me good, but I still found the remoter darkness of the place, and its perfect stillness, too stimulating for the imagination. The echoing of the stir and crackling of the fire was no sort of comfort to me. The shadow in the alcove at the end in particular had that undefinable quality of a presence,. that odd suggestion of a lurking, living thing, that comes so easily in silence and solitude. At last, to reassure myself, I walked with a candle into it, and satisfied myself that there was nothing tangible there. I stood that candle upon the floor of the alcove, and left it in that position.

By this time I was in a state of considerable nervous tension, although to my reason there was no adequate cause for the condition. My mind, however, was perfectly clear. I postulated quite unreservedly that nothing supernatural could happen, and to pass the time I began to string some rhymes together, Ingoldsby fashion[1], of the original legend of the place. A few I spoke aloud, but the echoes were not pleasant. For the same reason I also abandoned, after a time, a conversation with myself upon the impossibility of ghosts and haunting. My mind reverted to the three old and distorted people downstairs, and I tried to keep it upon that topic. The sombre reds and blacks of the room troubled me; even with seven candles the place was merely dim. The one in the alcove flared in a draught, and the fire's flickering kept the shadows and penumbra

---

[1] rhymes in a lively fashion. 'The Ingoldsby Legends' (1837) was a collection of popular rhymes.

perpetually shifting and stirring. Casting about for a remedy, I recalled the candles I had seen in the passage, and, with a slight effort, walked out into the moonlight, carrying a candle and leaving the door open, and presently returned with as many as ten. These I put in various knick-knacks of china with which the room was sparsely adorned, lit and placed where the shadows had lain deepest, some on the floor, some in the window recesses, until at last my seventeen candles were so arranged that not an inch of the room but had the direct light of at least one of them. It occurred to me that when the ghost came, I could warn him not to trip over them. The room was now quite brightly illuminated. There was something very cheery and reassuring in these little streaming flames, and snuffing them gave me an occupation, and afforded a helpful sense of the passage of time.

Even with that, however, the brooding expectation of the vigil weighed heavily upon me. It was after midnight that the candle in the alcove suddenly went out, and the black shadow sprang back to its place there. I did not see the candle go out; I simply turned and saw that the darkness was there, as one might start and see the unexpected presence of a stranger. 'By Jove!' said I aloud; 'that draught's a strong one!' and taking the matches from the table, I walked across the room in a leisurely manner to relight the corner again. My first match would not strike, and as I succeeded with the second, something seemed to blink on the wall before me. I turned my head involuntarily, and saw that the two candles on the little table by the fireplace were extinguished. I rose at once to my feet.

'Odd!' I said. 'Did I do that myself in a flash of absent-mindedness?'

I walked back, relit one, and as I did so, I saw the

candle in the right sconce of one of the mirrors wink
and go right out, and almost immediately its companion
followed it. There was no mistake about it. The flame
vanished, as if the wicks had been suddenly nipped between a finger and thumb, leaving the wick neither
glowing nor smoking, but black. While I stood gaping,
the candle at the foot of the bed went out, and the
shadows seemed to take another step towards me.

'This won't do!' said I, and first one and then
another candle on the mantelshelf followed.

'What's up?' I cried, with a queer high note getting
into my voice somehow. At that the candle on the
wardrobe went out, and the one I had relit in the alcove
followed.

'Steady on!' I said. 'These candles are wanted,'
speaking with a half-hysterical facetiousness, and
scratching away at a match the while for the mantel
candlesticks. My hands trembled so much that twice I
missed the rough paper of the matchbox. As the mantel
emerged from darkness again, two candles in the
remoter end of the window were eclipsed. But with the
same match I also relit the larger mirror candles, and
those on the floor near the doorway, so that for the moment I seemed to gain on the extinctions. But then in
a volley there vanished four lights at once in different
corners of the room, and I struck another match in
quivering haste, and stood hesitating whither to take
it.

As I stood undecided, an invisible hand seemed to
sweep out the two candles on the table. With a cry of
terror, I dashed at the alcove, then into the corner, and
then into the window, relighting three, as two more
vanished by the fireplace; then, perceiving a better way,
I dropped the matches on the iron-bound deedbox in
the corner, and caught up the bedroom candlestick.

With this I avoided the delay of striking matches; but for all that the steady process of extinction went on, and the shadows I feared and fought against returned, and crept in upon me, first a step gained on this side of me and then on that. It was like a ragged storm-cloud sweeping out the stars. Now and then one returned for a minute, and was lost again. I was now almost frantic with the horror of the coming darkness, and my self-possession deserted me. I leaped panting and dishevelled from candle to candle in a vain struggle against that remorseless advance.

I bruised myself on the thigh against the table, I sent a chair headlong, I stumbled and fell and whisked the cloth from the table in my fall. My candle rolled away from me, and I snatched another as I rose. Abruptly this was blown out, as I swung it off the table, by the wind of my sudden movement, and immediately the two remaining candles followed. But there was light still in the room, a red light that staved off the shadows from me. The fire! Of course I could still thrust my candle between the bars and relight it!

I turned to where the flames were still dancing between the glowing coals, and splashing red reflections upon the furniture, made two steps towards the grate, and incontinently the flames dwindled and vanished, the glow vanished, the reflections rushed together and vanished, and as I thrust the candle between the bars darkness closed upon me like the shutting of an eye, wrapped about me in a stifling embrace, sealed my vision, and crushed the last vestiges of reason from my brain. The candle fell from my hand. I flung out my arms in a vain effort to thrust that ponderous blackness away from me, and, lifting up my voice, screamed with all my might – once, twice, thrice. Then I think I must have staggered to my feet. I know I thought suddenly of the moonlit corridor, and, with my head bowed and my arms over my face, made a run for the door.

But I had forgotten the exact position of the door, and struck myself heavily against the corner of the bed. I staggered back, turned, and was either struck or struck myself against some other bulky furniture. I have a vague memory of battering myself thus, to and fro in the darkness, of a cramped struggle, and of my own wild crying as I darted to and fro, of a heavy blow at last upon my forehead, a horrible sensation of falling that lasted an age, of my last frantic effort to keep my footing, and then I remember no more.

I opened my eyes in daylight. My head was roughly bandaged, and the man with the withered arm was watching my face. I looked about me, trying to remember what had happened, and for a space I could not recollect. I rolled my eyes into the corner, and saw the old woman, no longer abstracted, pouring out some drops of medicine from a little blue phial into a glass. 'Where am I?' I asked; 'I seem to remember you, and yet I cannot remember who you are.'

They told me then, and I heard of the haunted red room as one who hears a tale. 'We found you at dawn,' said he, 'and there was blood on your forehead and lips.'

It was very slowly I recovered my memory of my experience. 'You believe now,' said the old man, 'that the room is haunted?' He spoke no longer as one who greets an intruder, but as one who grieves for a broken friend.

'Yes,' said I; 'the room is haunted.'

'And you have seen it. And we, who have lived here all our lives, have never set eyes upon it. Because we have never dared . . . Tell us, is it truly the old earl who — '

'No,' said I; 'it is not.'

'I told you so,' said the old lady, with the glass in her hand. 'It is his poor young countess who was frightened — '

'It is not,' I said. 'There is neither ghost of earl nor ghost of countess in that room, there is no ghost there at all; but worse, far worse — '

'Well?' they said.

'The worst of all the things that haunt poor mortal man,' said I; 'and that is, in all its nakedness – *Fear!* Fear that will not have light nor sound, that will not bear with reason, that deafens and darkens and over-whelms. It followed me through the corridor, it fought against me in the room — '

I stopped abruptly. There was an interval of silence. My hand went up to my bandages.

Then the man with the shade sighed and spoke. 'That is it,' said he. 'I knew that was it. A power of darkness. To put such a curse upon a woman! It lurks there al-ways. You can feel it even in the daytime, even of a bright summer's day, in the hangings, in the curtains, keeping behind you however you face about. In the dusk it creeps along the corridor and follows you, so that you dare not turn. There is Fear in that room of hers – black Fear, and there will be – so long as this house of sin endures.'

Andrina

George Mackay Brown

George Mackay Brown

Andrina

Andrina comes to see me every afternoon in winter, just before it gets dark. She lights my lamp, sets the peat fire in a blaze, sees that there is enough water in my bucket that stands on the wall niche. If I have a cold (which isn't often, I'm a tough old seaman) she fusses a little, puts an extra peat or two on the fire, fills a stone hot-water bottle, puts an old thick jersey about my shoulders.

That good Andrina – as soon as she has gone, after her occasional ministrations to keep pleurisy or pneumonia away – I throw the jersey from my shoulders and mix myself a toddy, whisky and hot water and sugar. The hot water bottle in the bed will be cold long before I climb into it, round about midnight: having read my few chapters of Conrad.

Towards the end of February last year I did get a very bad cold, the worst for years. I woke up, shuddering, one morning, and crawled between fire and cupboard, gasping like a fish out of water, to get a breakfast ready. (Not that I had an appetite.) There was a stone lodged somewhere in my right lung, that blocked my breath.

I forced down a few tasteless mouthfuls, and drank hot ugly tea. There was nothing to do after that but get back to bed with my book. Reading was no pleasure either – my head was a block of pulsing wood.

'Well,' I thought, 'Andrina'll be here in five or six

hours' time. She won't be able to do much for me. This cold, or flu, or whatever it is, will run its course. Still, it'll cheer me to see the girl.'

Andrina did not come that afternoon. I expected her with the first cluster of shadows: the slow lift of the latch, the low greeting, the 'tut-tut' of sweet disapproval at some of the things she saw as soon as the lamp was burning . . . I was, though, in that strange fatalistic mood that sometimes accompanies a fever, when a man doesn't really care what happens. If the house was to go on fire, he might think, 'What's this, flames?' and try to save himself: but it wouldn't horrify or thrill him.

I accepted that afternoon, when the window was blackness at last with a first salting of stars, that for some reason or another Andrina couldn't come. I fell asleep again.

I woke up. A grey light at the window. My throat was dry – there was a fire in my face – my head was more throbbingly wooden than ever. I got up, my feet flashing with cold pain on the stone floor, drank a cup of water, and climbed back into bed. My teeth actually clacked and chattered in my head for five minutes or more – a thing I had only read about before.

I slept again, and woke up just as the winter sun was making brief stained glass of sea and sky. It was, again, Andrina's time. Today there were things she could do for me: get aspirin from the shop, surround my greyness with three or four very hot bottles, mix the strongest toddy in the world. A few words from her would be like a bell-buoy to a sailor in a hopeless fog. She did not come.

She did not come again on the third afternoon.

I woke, tremblingly, like a ghost in a hollow stone. It was black night. Wind soughed in the chimney. There was, from time to time, spatters of rain against the window. It was the longest night of my life. I experienced, over again, some of the dull and sordid events of my life; one certain episode was repeated again and again like an ancient gramophone record being put on time after time, and a rusty needle scuttling over worn wax. The shameful images broke and melted at last into sleep. Love had been killed but many ghosts had been awakened.

When I woke up I heard, for the first time in four days, the sound of a voice. It was Stanley the postman speaking to the dog of Bighouse. 'There now, isn't that loud big words to say so early? It's just a letter for Minnie, a drapery catalogue. There's a good boy, go and tell Minnie I have a love letter for her . . . Is that you, Minnie? I thought old Ben here was going to tear me in pieces then. Yes, Minnie, a fine morning, it is that . . .'

I have never liked that postman — a servile lickspittle to anyone he thinks is of consequence in the island — but that morning he came past my window like a messenger of light. He opened the door without knocking (I am a person of small consequence). He said, 'Letter from a long distance, skipper.' He put the letter on the chair nearest the door. I was shaping my mouth to say, 'I'm not very well. I wonder . . . ' If words did come out of my mouth, they must have been whispers, a ghost appeal. He looked at the dead fire and the closed window. He said, 'Phew! It's fuggy in here, skipper. You want to get some fresh air . . .' Then he went, closing the door behind him. (He would not, as I had briefly hoped, be taking word to Andrina, or the doctor down in the village.)

I imagined, until I drowsed again, Captain Scott writing his few last words in the Antarctic tent.

In a day or two, of course, I was as right as rain; a tough old salt like me isn't killed off that easily.

But there was a sense of desolation on me. It was as if I had been betrayed – deliberately kicked when I was down. I came almost to the verge of self-pity. Why had my friend left me in my bad time?

Then good sense asserted itself. 'Torvald, you old fraud,' I said to myself. 'What claim have you got, anyway, on a winsome twenty-year-old? None at all. Look at it this way, man – you've had a whole winter of her kindness and consideration. She brought a lamp into your dark time: ever since the Harvest Home when (like a fool) you had too much whisky and she supported you home and rolled you unconscious into bed . . . Well, for some reason or another, Andrina hasn't been able to come these last few days. I'll find out, today, the reason.'

It was high time for me to get to the village. There was not a crust or scraping of butter or jam in the cupboard. The shop was also the post office – I had to draw two weeks' pension. I promised myself a pint or two in the pub, to wash the last of that sickness out of me.

It struck me, as I trudged those two miles, that I knew nothing about Andrina at all. I had never asked, and she had said nothing. What was her father? Had she sisters and brothers? Even the district of the island where she lived had never cropped up in our talks. It was sufficient that she came every evening, soon after sunset, and performed her quiet ministrations, and lingered awhile; and left a peace behind – a sense that everything in the house was pure, as if it had stood with open doors and windows at the heart of a clean summer wind.

Yet the girl had never done, all last winter, asking me questions about myself – all the good and bad and exciting things that had happened to me. Of course I told her this and that. Old men love to make their past vivid and significant, to stand in relation to a few trivial events in as fair and bold a light as possible. To add spice to those bits of autobiography, I let on to have been a reckless wild daring lad – a known and somewhat feared figure in many a port from Hong Kong to Durban to San Francisco. I presented to her a character somewhere between Captain Cook and Captain Hook.

And the girl loved those pieces of mingled fiction and fact; turning the wick of my lamp down a little to make everything more mysterious, stirring the peats into new flowers of flame . . .

One story I did not tell her completely. It is the episode in my life that hurts me whenever I think of it (which is rarely, for that time is locked up and the key dropped deep in the Atlantic: but it haunted me – as I hinted – during my recent illness).

On her last evening at my fireside I did, I know, let drop a hint or two to Andrina – a few half-ashamed half-boastful fragments. Suddenly, before I had finished – as if she could foresee and suffer the end – she had put a white look and cold kiss on my cheek, and gone out at the door; as it turned out, for the last time.

Hurt or not, I will mention it here and now. You who look and listen are not Andrina – to you it will seem a tale of crude country manners: a mingling of innocence and heartlessness.

In the island, fifty years ago, a young man and a young woman came together. They had known each other all their lives up to then, of course – they had sat in the school room together – but on one particular day in early summer this boy from one croft and this girl from another distant croft looked at each other with new eyes.

After the midsummer dance in the barn of the big house, they walked together across the hill through the lingering enchantment of twilight – it is never dark then – and came to the rocks and the sand and sea just as the sun was rising. For an hour and more they lingered, tranced creatures indeed, beside those bright sighings and swirlings. Far in the north-east the springs of day were beginning to surge up.

It was a tale soaked in the light of a single brief summer. The boy and the girl lived, it seemed, on each other's heartbeats. Their parents' crofts were miles apart, but they contrived to meet, as if by accident, most days; at the crossroads, in the village shop, on the side of the hill. But really these places were too earthy and open – there were too many windows – their feet drew secretly night after night to the beach with its bird-cries, its cave, its changing waters. There no one disturbed their communings – the shy touches of hand and mouth – the words that were nonsense but that became in his mouth sometimes a sweet mysterious music – 'Sigrid'.

The boy – his future, once this idyll of a summer was ended, was to go to the university in Aberdeen and there study to be a man of security and position and some leisure – an estate his crofting ancestors had never known.

No such door was to open for Sigrid – she was bound to the few family acres – the digging of peat – the making of butter and cheese. But for a short time only. Her place would be beside the young man with whom she shared her breath and heartbeats, once he had gained his teacher's certificate. They walked day after day beside the shining beckoning waters.

But one evening, at the cave, towards the end of that summer, when the corn was taking a first burnish, she had something urgent to tell him – a tremulous perilous secret thing. And at once the summertime spell was broken. He shook his head. He looked away. He looked at her again as if she were some slut who had insulted him. She put out her hand to him, her mouth trembling. He thrust her away. He turned. He ran up the beach and along the sand-track to the road above; and the ripening fields gathered him soon and hid him from her.

And the girl was left alone at the mouth of the cave, with the burden of a greater more desolate mystery on her.

The young man did not go to any seat of higher learning. That same day he was at the emigration agents in Hamnavoe, asking for an urgent immediate passage to Canada or Australia or South Africa – anywhere.

Thereafter the tale became complicated and more cruel and pathetic still. The girl followed him as best she could to his transatlantic refuge a month or so later; only to discover that the bird had flown. He had signed on a ship bound for furthest ports, as an ordinary seaman: so she was told, and she was more utterly lost than ever.

That rootlessness, for the next half century, was to be his life: making salt circles about the globe, with no secure footage anywhere. To be sure, he studied his navigation manuals, he rose at last to be a ship's officer, and more. The barren years became a burden to him. There is a time, when white hairs come, to turn one's back on long and practised skills and arts, that have long since lost their savours. This the sailor did, and he set his course homeward to his island; hoping that fifty winters might have scabbed over an old wound.

And so it was, or seemed to be. A few remembered him vaguely. The name of a certain vanished woman – who must be elderly, like himself, now – he never mentioned, nor did he ever hear it uttered. Her parents' croft was a ruin, a ruckle of stones on the side of the hill. He climbed up to it one day and looked at it coldly. No sweet ghost lingered at the end of the house, waiting for a twilight summons – 'Sigrid . . .'

I got my pension cashed, and a basket full of provisions, in the village shop. Tina Stewart the postmistress knew everybody and everything; all the shifting subtle web of relationship in the island. I tried devious approaches with her. What was new or strange in the island? Had anyone been taken suddenly ill? Had anybody – a young woman, for example – had to leave the island suddenly, for whatever reason? The hawk eye of Miss Stewart regarded me long and hard. No, said she, she had never known the island quieter. Nobody had come or gone. 'Only yourself, Captain Torvald, has been bedridden, I hear. You better take good care of yourself, you all alone up there. There's still a greyness in your face . . .' I said I was sorry to take her time up. Somebody had mentioned a name – Andrina – to me, in a certain connection. It was a matter of no importance. Could Miss Stewart, however, tell me which farm or croft this Andrina came from?

Tina looked at me a long while, then shook her head. There was nobody of that name – woman or girl or child – in the island; and there never had been, to her certain knowledge.

I paid for my messages, with trembling fingers, and left.

I felt the need of a drink. At the bar counter stood Isaac Irving the landlord. Two fishermen stood at the far end, next the fire, drinking their pints and playing dominoes.

I said, after the third whisky, 'Look, Isaac, I suppose the whole island knows that Andrina – that girl – has been coming all winter up to my place, to do a bit of cleaning and washing and cooking for me. She hasn't been for a week now and more. Do you know if there's anything the matter with her?' (What I dreaded to hear was that Andrina had suddenly fallen in love; her little rockpools of charity and kindness drowned in that huge incoming flood; and cloistered herself against the time of her wedding.)

Isaac looked at me as if I was out of my mind. 'A young woman,' said he. 'A young woman up at your house? A home help, is she? I didn't know you had a home help. How many whiskies did you have before you came here, skipper, eh?' And he winked at the two grinning fishermen over by the fire.

I drank down my fourth whisky and prepared to go.

'Sorry, skipper,' Isaac Irving called after me. 'I think you must have imagined that girl, whatever her name is, when the fever was on you. Sometimes that happens. The only women I saw when I had the flu were hags and witches. You're lucky, skipper – a honey like Andrina!'

I was utterly bewildered. Isaac Irving knows the island and its people, if anything, even better than Tina Stewart. And he is a kindly man, not given to making fools of the lost and the delusion-ridden.

Going home, March airs were moving over the island. The sky, almost overnight, was taller and bluer. Daffodils trumpeted, silently, the entry of spring from ditches here and there. A young lamb danced, all four feet in the air at once.

I found, lying on the table, unopened, the letter that had been delivered three mornings ago. There was an Australian postmark. It had been posted in late October.

'I followed your young flight from Selskay half round the world, and at last stopped here in Tasmania, knowing that it was useless for me to go any farther. I have kept a silence too, because I had such regard for you that I did not want you to suffer as I had, in many ways, over the years. We are both old, maybe I am writing this in vain, for you might never have returned to Selskay; or you might be dust or salt. I think, if you are still alive and (it may be) lonely, that what I will write might gladden you, though the end of it is sadness, like so much of life. Of your child – our child – I do not say anything, because you did not wish to acknowledge her. But that child had, in her turn, a daughter, and I think I have seen such sweetness but rarely. I thank you that you, in a sense (though unwillingly), gave that light and goodness to my age. She would have been a lamp in your winter, too, for often I spoke to her about you and that long-gone summer we shared, which was, to me at least, such a wonder. I told her nothing of the end of that time, that you and some others thought to be shameful. I told her only things that came sweetly from my mouth. And she would say, often, 'I wish I knew that grandfather of mine. Gran, do you think he's lonely? I think he would be glad of somebody to make him a pot of tea and see to his fire. Some day I'm going to Scotland and I'm going to knock on his door, wherever he lives, and I'll do things for him. Did you love him very much, gran?

He must be a good person, that old sailor, ever to have been loved by you. I *will* see him. I'll hear the old stories from his own mouth. Most of all, of course, the love story – for you, gran, tell me nothing about that . . .' I am writing this letter, Bill, to tell you that this can never now be. Our granddaughter Andrina died last week, suddenly, in the first stirrings of spring . . .'

Later, over the fire, I thought of the brightness and burgeoning and dew that visitant had brought across the threshold of my latest winter, night after night; and of how she had always come with the first shadows and the first star; but there, where she was dust, a new time was brightening earth and sea.

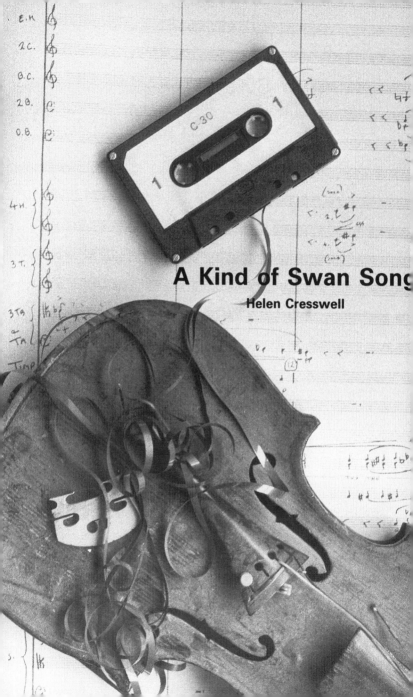

A Kind of Swan Song

Helen Cresswell

Helen Cresswell

A Kind of Swan Song

When I say that Lisa was someone special, right from the beginning, I expect that you will smile. *All* mothers think their children are special – and so they are, of course. In my case, Lisa was my only child, and so you will think that perhaps it is only natural that I should think her special. And when I tell you that my husband (who was a violinist with a well-known symphony orchestra) died when she was only a few months old, then you will quite understandably suspect me of exaggeration. I don't blame you. This is how it might seem.

But I must insist – Lisa *was* special. And perhaps it is partly because it is important to me that other people should realise this too, that I am now writing her story. It will not take long. She was only eight when she died.

The other reason I feel bound to tell her story is because I want you to know, as certainly as I now do myself, that death is not the end, not a full stop.

'Ah,' I hear you say, 'but she is *bound* to say that. She had no one in the world but her little daughter, and she died. Now she is trying to convince herself that death is not the end of everything. It's understandable, but she can't expect *us* to believe that!'

To this I simply reply – 'Wait. Wait until you have heard my story. Then decide.'

At birth, Lisa was special to Peter and myself in exactly the same way as any other baby born to loving parents.

In our case, there was an extra dimension to our joy because we knew already that in Peter's case it was to be short-lived. We knew that he had only a few months, at most, to savour the delights of parenthood. He had had to leave the orchestra several weeks before her birth. And so, for those first few months of Lisa's life Peter was as close to her as any father can be. He would sit with her for hours, studying her tiny, peaceful face as if he wanted to imprint it on his heart forever. In the early days, before he grew too weak, he would bath her, change her, put her to bed.

And then he would play music to her, for hours on end. Not himself – he had sorrowfully put his violin away before her birth, but on tapes, and records. She would lie there kicking on the rug to the strains of Bach and Mozart, songs of Schubert and grand opera.

Sometimes I would laugh and say that I thought it all rather beyond the grasp of a baby, and that we should be playing her nursery rhymes instead. But he would say, quite seriously, 'That baby may not be able to talk, yet, but she can hear. She is listening, the whole time, trying to make a pattern of this strange new world she has entered. If what she hears is joyful, if she hears harmony then all her life long she will seek out joy and harmony for herself. Believe me, Martha, I know that I am right.'

Even at the time I acknowledged that what he said might be true. Now, I know that it was.

I don't want to give the impression by this that we were too serious about things, or that Lisa had a strange start in life. Like any young parents we romped and played with her, looked for ways of making her smile or, better still, laugh. And we sang nursery rhymes as well. But I honestly think that the times she loved best, the times when she seemed happiest, were when she was lying there listening to music – especially songs. There was a special peaceful, wondering look she seemed to wear when she heard a beautiful human voice singing great music.

I don't want to exaggerate this – it is how I remember it, but then perhaps my memory of that time is not very reliable. It is a strange thing for a woman to watch her child blossom and at the same time her husband, the father, fading. Joy and sorrow could hardly be more poignantly interwoven.

Peter refused to let me grieve openly, and himself would show no sign of bitterness that he must soon leave us.

'I want there to be no shadows over her,' he said. 'Let her be shaped by music, not by sorrow.'

Strangely, afterwards, when she was four or five, she would insist that she remembered Peter, though she could not really have done so.

'He was always smiling,' she would say. And that was certainly true, so far as she was concerned. If there were times when he allowed his smile to fade, it was never in her presence.

He died when she was just over eight months old – in time to see her crawling, but before she took her first steps.

'Promise you will keep playing her music,' he said before he died. And of course I promised. And that was another strange thing.

In those unreal, nightmarish days after he died, Lisa grew pale and quiet. It was as if she, too, were mourning. Then, coming back into the house after the funeral, drained and weary, I was suddenly aware of the great silence and absence. It occurred to me that since Peter died, I had played no music. I went and put on a record – one of his favourites, from Haydn's 'Creation'. As the pure, triumphant notes swelled about me, I lay back in a chair and surrendered myself to it. Then, beyond that marvellous music, I heard, in a pause, another music, another voice – Lisa's.

I hurried into the next room where she lay, as I thought, sleeping. Instead, she lay there wide eyed and round mouthed, too. Her whole tiny being seemed intent on the sounds that she was making with such seriousness, such concentration – Lisa was singing.

Very well – perhaps she was not. Perhaps she was simply cooing, crooning, as babies do. But to me, in my overwrought condition, it seemed that she was singing, herself joining in Haydn's great celebratory hymn. I remember that my tears, all at once released, splashed down onto her face, and that I gathered her up and took her with me, and she lay against me while we listened together.

Some children walk before they talk, some the other way round. Lisa, I swear, sang before she did either. I have the courage to say this, in the light of what came after. I did not merely imagine that Lisa was a child of music. She quite simply, and unarguably, was.

At first it was only I who knew it, and who could hardly believe it when I heard that infant voice playing with scales as other children play with bricks. (She did that, too. She was in every way exactly like all other children of her age. Only this was different – music ran in her veins.)

Then, as she grew older and we went to playgroups, others would remark on the purity and the pitch of her voice, and noticed that she had only to hear a song once to know it off by heart.

'She takes after her father,' they all said.

It was true. But only I knew that she was composing music, as well as singing it. She would lie in bed after

I had tucked her in for the night, her voice tracing its own melodies in the darkness. Sometimes even I, her own mother, would give a little shiver.

The word 'genius' is not an easy one to come to terms with. Every mother, as I have said believes her own child to be special. But I do not think that any mother is looking for genius. It is rather a frightening thing, for ordinary people. We admit that it exists – but at a great distance, and in other people (preferably long since dead!).

At two Lisa was picking out tunes on the piano; at three she was playing both piano and violin. But it was the singing that mattered, I knew that. I watched her grow and develop with a delight tinged with sadness. I knew even then that the days of our closeness were numbered. Soon the world would discover her, and then the music would no longer be our shared secret.

When she was only four photographs of her were beginning to appear in the papers, under headlines such as 'Child Prodigy wins Premier Award at Festival' and 'Little Lisa Triumphs Again'.

I don't want you to think that she was in any way strange. She was exactly like every other little girl in most ways. She loved reading, roller-skating and using her computer. When she started school, her marks were average. It was only the music that set her apart.

When she was five all kinds of renowned people – professors and teachers of music – began to visit us.

'Soon,' I thought, 'they will take her away from me.'

They wanted me, even then, to send her away to a special school, where her gift could be nurtured.

'It doesn't need nurturing,' I told them. It is natural. It will flower of its own accord.'

They went away again, but I knew that it would not be for long. I knew, too, that what I had told them was only partly true. *Any* gift needs the right nourishment, just as a rare and fragile plant.

Lisa herself began to grow away from me. Not in the things that mattered – the things between mother and daughter. In those things we were always close. We teased each other a lot and sometimes, even then, it would seem as if she were older than I was.

'Dear goose mother!' she would say, if I forgot something, or made a mistake. It became her pet name for me.

At six they tried to take her away again, and again I resisted.

'It's too soon,' I said. 'She's too young. Leave her with me a little longer, then she can go.'

This time, when they had gone, I thought I could sense a sadness in her, a disappointment. I thought perhaps that I was being selfish, over-possessive. And so when they came again, begging me, almost, to send her away, I gave in.

Her delight when she heard the news hurt me, and she must have seen this.

'I'll still be home in the holidays, dear goose mother,' she told me. 'Don't be sad, or you'll spoil it for me.'

So I tried to look glad, for her sake. During those last few months together before she went away, I gathered her music together, to comfort me in her absence. Every song she composed I made her sing into a microphone so that I could record it. I recorded her playing the piano and the violin too, but it was the singing that mattered. We both knew that. When she sang, instrument and music were one, perfect and inviolable.

She was still only seven when she left for her new school. She was radiant. She was like a bride in beret and navy socks.

'No crying, goose mother,' she told me. 'We'll write to each other.'

'And send me tapes,' I said. 'Please, Lisa. Don't let even a single song you make get away. Put it on tape. That way, we've got it forever.'

She smiled then with a curious wisdom.

'It's *making* the song that matters,' she said. *Nothing* gets away – ever.'

When she had gone, I *did* cry, as I knew I would, and I kept remembering those words. How could she *know*, I wondered, something that most people never learn in a lifetime?

I took a job – an interesting one, really – in a house belonging to the National Trust, and open to visitors. Even so, that first term dragged. Most evenings I would sit and listen to the tapes we had made that summer. And at weekends I'd go shopping – looking for little things to put in her stocking. Lisa still believed (at least, I think she did) in Father Christmas.

By mid-December she was home. For a day or so we were a little strange together, and then it was as though she had never been away. One evening, we turned on the television to see a programme of carols composed by children. It was a competition, and these were the winning entries. When it was over, Lisa said quietly, 'Next year, goose mother, *I* shall make a carol!'

That was all. It was so slight a thing that, were it not for what followed, I doubt whether I should have remembered it. Lisa, after all, had been making songs almost all her life. What was more natural than that she should make a carol?

Christmas and the New Year came and went. This time, when she left for school, the wrench was not so painful. We can become in time accustomed to most things – even to the absence of those we love. It all seemed inevitable, and for me, it was also part of the promise I had made to Peter before he died.

Lisa's letters came every week – badly spelt, and full of the things she was doing, the music she was making. They were full, too, of the ordinary things – requests for clothes that were all the rage, for stamps to swap and posters for her room. That term passed, and the next. In the summer I took a cottage in the Lakes, and we spent most of the time walking and cycling. We were well on the way to establishing a pattern to our lives.

It was sometimes hard to remember that she was still only eight years old. And we never talked about what she would 'do' when she was 'grown up'. Looking back, I think that this was because she was already what she was meant to be. She was all the time in a process of becoming, and this was all that was necessary. She knew it herself.

'It's *making* the song that matters,' she had said, over a year ago.

Again I waved her off to the start of a new school year. This time the ache was not so bad. I even registered for evening classes in Italian, and went out occasionally with friends to the theatre, or for a meal. But Lisa still made the tapes, and I still played them, hour upon hour. Now, she was beginning to write her own words to the music. One day I received a cassette with a song called 'Goose Mother' and I felt so happy and so honoured that I actually taped it again, on to another cassette, for fear that it might get lost or damaged. Even as I did so, I seemed to hear her saying, 'It's *making* the song that matters'. I smiled wryly.

'For you, perhaps,' I thought. 'But for the rest of us, who can only listen, it's the song itself that counts.'

In November I was surprised by Lisa calling me on the telephone. This she had done only once before – to inform me that she had chicken pox, but there was no need to worry, and proudly announce the number of spots she had.

'Listen,' she said, 'I've made a carol!'

'A carol?' I echoed.

'Remember – that competition we saw? And listen – Davey's going home, for the weekend, and I can go with him! So you and I can record it together – on our own piano!'

'Darling, that's wonderful!' I said. 'But . . .'

'Look – his mother's coming to fetch us in the car. I'll be home Friday, at around six. Can't stop now – bye!'

That was all. It was Tuesday – three days to get used to the wonderful fact that Lisa was coming home. I had quite forgotten (how could I?) that during their first year children at the school were not allowed to go home during termtime, but that this rule was lifted after that.

I spent the interim pleasurably shopping for Lisa's favourite food (not a difficult task; this being mainly a variation on chicken) and bought a new duvet cover for her bedroom. By half-past-five on the Friday I was fidgeting in the kitchen – opening and re-opening the oven door to check on the degree of brownness of chicken and potatoes, wondering whether I should start thawing the chocolate mousse.

At quarter-to-six I remembered that I hadn't any fizzy lemonade – her favourite drink, and one not allowed at school. I hesitated.

'I'll write a note,' I thought, 'and pin it on the door. I'll only be five minutes.'

Accordingly I wrote 'Back in five minutes' and pinned it on the door and set off. There were no shops nearby. I took the car and made for the nearest late-night supermarket. The traffic was dense, irritatingly slow. I had forgotten what Friday night rush hours were like. At one point, I almost seized the opportunity to turn round and go home without the lemonade. But, I reflected, people rarely arrived on time, especially at the weekends. I carried on.

It was nearly quarter-past-six when I arrived back. In the space my own car had occupied only half-an-hour previously, was another. It was a police car. I drew alongside it, oblivious to the hooting behind me. Two figures, a policeman and a policewoman, were standing on the steps up to the front door.

I wrenched open the door and got out. I was telling myself to keep calm. My knees were trembling.

'What − what is it?'

They turned. Their faces were young, worried, pitying.

'Mrs Viner?'

I nodded.

'Perhaps we can . . .?'

I hardly remember what happened then exactly. Somehow I was inside, somehow I was sitting in my usual chair facing the fire and a voice was talking to me. It was a sympathetic voice, its owner reluctant to give me the news. 'Motorway . . . wet surface . . . central reservation . . . lorry . . . ' The words washed over me. What they were telling me was that Lisa was dead. She had been killed, along with her friend and his mother, on the motorway.

They were very kind. The young woman made me a cup of tea and switched off the oven. Before they left they stood looking at me uncertainly, at a loss. They didn't know what to say.

'Funny thing,' said the policeman, 'we'd been there on the steps ten minutes before you came.'

I said nothing.

'Could've sworn there was someone in here,' he went on. 'Could hear someone singing – a kid, it sounded like.'

'We wondered if the radio had been left on,' the girl added.

'And now I come to think of it,' he said, 'the radio *wasn't* on. Or the telly. Funny, that . . . '

'Yes, funny,' I said. 'Thank you. Thank you both very much. I think – I think I want to be alone now.'

They hesitated.

'Sure you'll be all right?'

'Sure.'

They went. The door closed and I was alone. I sat there for I don't know how long. I was seeing Lisa, hearing her, trying to tell myself that I would never see or hear her again. I couldn't cry. I just sat, dry-eyed, remembering.

In the end, after a long dark age, I got up. Mechanically I began turning things off, locking up for the night. The front door, the back, check the oven – still containing the chicken and crisp potatoes – switch off lights, pull out the plug of the TV . . .

I stopped. All the lights but one were out. There, glowing in the darkness, were the red and green lights of the stereo deck and cassette recorder. There was a very faint hum. My mind was dense, confused. I had set *up* the system, that very afternoon, all ready to record the carol. The blank cassette was in place, I had carefully checked the sound levels. *And then I had switched it off.*

I remembered doing it. I had actually thought of the way Peter had always chided me for leaving things on – especially the cassette recorder. He had lectured me about the damage it might do.

I advanced towards the deck. Hesitantly, I pressed

the PLAY switch. There came only a faint hissing. Then, hardly knowing why I did so, I pressed REWIND. *The tape rewound.* It stopped with a click.

'But it was a new cassette,' I thought. 'Brand new.'

I stood there for a long time in the dim remaining light. Then I pressed another key – PLAY.

The room filled with sound. A voice – Lisa's voice, pure and sweet, sang:

On a far midnight,

Long, long ago . . .

There was no accompaniment, no piano, just that young, miraculous voice, singing of that long-ago miracle that Christmas celebrates.

I stood dazed, listening. Then, when at last the carol ended, I heard – or thought I heard (it certainly was not there on the tape, afterwards) – 'There, dear goose mother! I told you – it's *making* the song that matters!'

And I knew that this was her last present to me. It was not for her own sake, but for mine, that the carol was there, locked for all time, on tape.

I sent that tape to the contest. It won. The presenter said, 'It is with great sadness that we have to tell you that Lisa, aged eight, died tragically in a car accident, just after she had recorded this carol for our contest. It was to be her swan song.'

The Man Who Didn't Believe in Ghosts

Sorche Nic Leodhas

Sorche Nic Leodhas

The Man Who Didn't Believe in Ghosts

In a town not far from Edinburgh there was a house that was said to be haunted. It wasn't the sort of house you'd think would attract a ghost at all. It was only a two-storey cottage with a garret, and it was far too neat and pretty for ghosts to care much about. The outside walls of it were painted white and its casement windows had diamond-shaped panes to them. There was a climbing rose trained over the front door, and there was a flower garden before the house and a kitchen garden behind it, with a pear tree and an apple tree and a small green lawn. Who'd ever think that a ghost would choose to bide in a place like that? But folks did say it was haunted, all the same.

The house had belonged to an old lawyer with only one child, a daughter. Folk old enough to remember her still say that there never was another lass as bonny as her in the town. The old man loved her dearly but she died early. There was an old sad story told about her being in love with the son of an old laird who did not favour the match. The poor lad died of a fever while they were still courting, and not long after she died too – folk said of a broken heart.

After that the old man lived alone in the house, with a woman coming in each day to take care of it. There wasn't a word said about ghosts in the old man's time. He'd not have put up with it for a minute.

When the old lawyer died, there was nobody left that was kin to him but a second cousin several times removed. So to keep the property in the family, the old man left all he had to the cousin, including the house, of course.

The young man was grateful, but as he was not married, he had little use for a house. The lodgings he was living in suited him fine. So he put the renting of the house into an agent's hands. The rent money would make a nice little nest egg against the time when he decided he would like to get married. When that time came he'd want the house for himself.

It was the folks the agent found to live in the house that started all the talk about ghosts. At first they were very well pleased with the house, but as time passed they began to notice queer things were happening in it. Doors would open and close again, with nobody at all near them. When the young wife was dusting the spare bedroom, she heard drawers being pulled open and shut again behind her, but when she turned about to look, no one at all was there.

Things were lifted and put down again before the tenants' very eyes, but they couldn't see who was lifting them or putting them down. They came to have the feeling there was somebody always in the house with them. Of course, they tried to be sensible about it, but it gave them a terribly eerie feeling. As for getting a maid to stay, it couldn't be done! The maids all said that they felt that someone was always looking over their shoulders while they worked, and every time they set something down, it got itself moved to another place. They wouldn't take it upon themselves to say why, but they'd take whatever pay was coming to them, and go. And they did.

The end of the tenants' stay in the house came upon

the day when the young wife came into the sitting-room to find her wee lad rolling his ball across the floor. Every time the ball reached the middle of the room it seemed to turn and roll itself back to him, as if someone who couldn't be seen were playing with him. But when he looked up at his mother and laughed and said 'Bonny lady!' 'twas more than she could bear. She caught him up in her arms and ran out of the door to one of the neighbours, and no one could persuade her to set foot in the house again. So her husband went to the agent and told him they were sorry, but the way things were, they'd have to give up the house.

The young man to whom the house had been left was a very matter-of-fact young fellow. He didn't believe in ghosts. He was quite put out because the story had got round that there were ghosts in the house. Of course, the young couple who had lived there couldn't be depended on not to talk about what had happened. It wouldn't have been according to human nature for them to keep quiet about it. What made it awkward was that by this time the young man had found a lass he wanted to marry, but unfortunately she had heard the story. And she did believe in ghosts.

She said that she loved him dearly and would like very much to marry him. But she told him flatly that she could never, *never* bring herself to live in a haunted house.

Then the young man told her that he would go and live in the house himself, just to prove that there were no ghosts in it. Anyway, he didn't believe in ghosts. So he left his lodgings and moved in and got himself settled comfortably in his house.

Well, the doors did open and close of themselves, but that didn't daunt him. He just took them off their hinges and rehung them. They went on opening and closing just the same, but he said that was only because of a flaw in the walls.

He had to admit to himself that he heard drawers opening and closing, and latches of cupboards clicking shut. There was a tinkling in the china closet, too, as if someone were moving the cups and plates about. And once or twice he thought he heard water running in the scullery. But when he looked, every tap was shut off tight. Besides, he knew there was no one but himself in the house. So he said that old houses were always full of queer noises because of the foundations settling, and paid them no more heed.

Even when a book he·had just closed and laid on the table opened itself again, and leaves turned over slowly as if someone were looking at them, he told himself that it was just a puff of wind from the window did it, although afterwards he remembered that the windows were closed at the time.

But still he didn't believe in ghosts.

So he went on living in the house and trying to persuade his sweetheart to marry him and come and live there with him. And, of course, to convince her that the house wasn't haunted at all. But he had no luck, for she wouldn't be persuaded.

Well, things went on in this unsatisfactory way until his summer holidays came round. He decided, now that he had the time for it, to do something he'd been meaning to do and never got round to. There were a lot of clothes in the attic that had belonged to the old lawyer and his daughter. It seemed sinful to leave them there to moulder away when some poor body'd be glad to have them. So what he was going to do was to pack them all up and send them to the Missionary Society where a good use would be found for them.

He went up to the garret and found some empty

boxes, and began to pack the clothes. They were all hanging in tall presses, ranged around the room. He packed the old lawyer's clothes first. There were a good many of them, suits and coats and boots and shoes, all of the best quality, to say nothing of a quantity of warm underclothing in boxes neatly stacked on the floors of the presses. When he had taken everything out and folded it neatly, he packed the boxes and set them out of his way, and turned to the press that held the dead lass's clothes. When he opened the first press there was a sound uncommonly like a sigh. It gave him a start for a moment, but then he laughed and told himself that it was only the silk of garments brushing against each other in the breeze made by the opening door. He began to take them out, one by one, and to fold them and gently lay them in the box he'd set ready for them. It made him feel a little bit sad and sentimental to be handling the dresses that had been worn by the pretty young thing who had died so young and so long ago.

He'd laid away five or six of them when he came to one frock that seemed strangely heavy for the material of which it was made. It was a light, crisp cotton sprigged with flowers still bright in spite of the years it had hung in the press. He thought that a dress like that should have had almost no weight at all, so he looked it over curiously. Perhaps a brooch or a buckle was the answer? Then he found a pocket set in the seam of the skirt, and in the pocket a small red book and a letter. It was a letter of the old style, with no envelope, and the dead girl's name and address on the outer folded sheet. He laid the dress aside and, taking his find to the low-set window, he sat down on the floor to read what he had found. He was not a man to read other people's letters and secrets, but something made him feel that it was right to do so now.

He read the letter first. It said:

My dear love:

Although they have not told me I know that I am very ill. It may be that we shall not meet again in this world. If I should die I beg of you make them promise that when you, too, are dead we shall lie together side by side.

Your true love

The young man sat for a while, thinking of the letter, wondering how it had come to the lass, remembering that he had heard that the old laird was hard set against the match. Then he took up the little red book and opened it. The little book was a sort of day-by-day diary with the date printed at the top of each page. It had begun as a sort of housekeeping journal. There was a lot in it about household affairs. There were records of sewing done, of jars of pickles and jams laid by, and about the house being turned out and cleaned from end to end, and such things. But through it all was the story of a young girl's heart. She told about meeting the laird's son, where they first met and when he first spoke to her of love and what they said and how they planned to marry as soon as the old laird could be persuaded to give his consent to the match. Although he was against it, they thought he might be brought over in time.

But they had no time, poor young things! Soon after, the diary told of the letter that John the Carrier had brought her, that had frightened her terribly. And the next page said only, 'My love is dead.' Page after page was empty after that. Then towards the end of the little book she had written: 'I know that I am going to die.

I asked my father today to promise to beg the laird to let me lie beside my love when I am dead, but he only turned away and would not answer. I am afraid his pride will not let him ask a favour of one who would not accept me into his family. But, oh my love, if he does not, I'll find a way to bring things right. I'll never rest until I do.'

And that was all.

The young man raised his eyes from the page and repeated thoughtfully. 'I'll never rest until I do.'

It was then and there that he began to believe in ghosts!

He put the diary and the letter into his pocket, and leaving everything just as it was in the garret, he went downstairs. The packing could wait for another day. He had something better to do. As he went he thought of the old lawyer living there day after day with the ghost of his dead daughter mutely beseeching him to do what his pride would never let him do.

'Well, I have no pride at all,' the young man said.

He packed a bag and put on his hat and coat, and started for the station. But as he went out of the door, he turned and put his head back in and called, 'Do not fret yourself any longer, lass! You can rest now, I'll find the way to bring things right.'

At the station he was fortunate enough to find a train that would take him where he wanted to go. When he got off the train he asked about the village for news of the laird. Och, the old laird was long dead, folk told him, and a rare old amadan that one was, though they shouldn't be saying it of the dead. But the new laird, him that was the old laird's nephew, had the estate now, and a finer man you'd not be finding should you search for a year and a day.

So up to the castle the young man went. When he

got there he found the new laird as reasonable a man as he could hope to find. So he gave him the letter and the diary and let him read the story for himself. Then he told him about his house and the ghost in it that would not rest until she had her way.

The old laird's nephew listened gravely, and at the end of the young man's story he sighed and said, 'Fifty years! Fifty long years! What a weary time to wait. Poor lass.'

The old laird's nephew believed in ghosts himself.

He called his solicitors at once and got them to work. They were so quick about it that by the time the young man got back home after paying a visit to the old laird's nephew who asked him to stay till all was settled, the two lovers were reunited at last and lay together side by side in the old laird's family tomb.

When he got home he could tell the minute he stepped through the door that there was no one there but himself. There was no more trouble with the doors, and the only sounds were the ordinary sounds that he made himself.

He finally persuaded the lass he wanted to marry to come for supper one night and bring along the old aunt she lived with. The aunt prided herself on having such a keen scent for ghosts that she could actually smell one if it was in a house. So they came, and as soon as they were all settled at the supper table the aunt looked all around the rooms and sniffed two or three times.

'Ghosts! Nonsense, my dear!' she said to the young man's lass firmly. 'There isn't a single ghost in this house. You may be sure I'd know at once, if there were!'

That satisfied the young lady. So, soon she and the young man were married. They lived together so happily in the house that folks completely forgot that it had ever been said that it was haunted. It didn't look at all like the kind of house that would ever have a ghost. Only the young man remembered.

He really did believe in ghosts, after all.

The Darkness under the Stairs

Lance Salway

Lance Salway

The Darkness under the Stairs

As soon as he stepped into the hall, Andrew knew at once that something was wrong. He couldn't tell what it was; he was simply aware of a dark wave of dread that rose to meet him the minute the front door was opened.

'Ah, there you are,' the woman said. 'You must be Andrew. We were wondering where you'd got to. I'm Carol Sharman.'

Andrew blinked at her, dazzled by the light in the hall. He wanted to turn and run, he wanted to get away from the house, but he couldn't. He had to stay.

'Your parents are in the sitting room,' Mrs Sharman went on. Then, as he hesitated still, 'Well, are you coming in or aren't you? I'm not going to hold the door open all night.'

'Sorry,' he muttered, and edged past her into the light, towards the darkness. He blinked again, and shuddered. Fear settled round him like a dark stifling blanket.

Ahead of him, a wide wooden staircase rose into shadows. To the left, he could hear voices, his mother's loud among them, behind a half-open door. He pushed it open and walked into the room.

'Ah, here he is at last,' his mother said, smiling at him from the sofa where she was sitting with his father.

'Sorry,' Andrew muttered again. 'I had some homework to finish.' He stared down at his feet and wished with all his heart that he'd stayed at home. He hadn't wanted to come in the first place. He could have met the new neighbours at any other time. But no, his mother had insisted that they all go next door together. The Sharmans had been kind enough to invite them all in for a drink so the very least he could do was accept graciously. And anyway, she said, just think how interesting it will be to see inside the house at last. After all these years.

'This is Mr Sharman, Andrew,' his mother said.

Andrew looked up into the pleasant face of a dark middle-aged man in glasses who nodded at him and said, 'Good to meet you, Andrew.'

'You've met *Mrs* Sharman, of course,' his mother went on. 'And then there's – it's Danny, isn't it? – yes, Danny.'

Andrew noticed for the first time a boy of about his own age sitting in a corner by the window. He had spiky red hair and pale blue eyes. 'Hi,' the boy said.

Andrew mumbled something and sat down abruptly on a chair by the door.

'I've just been telling Mr and Mrs Sharman about the house,' his mother went on brightly. 'How this is the first time we've ever been inside it. I've explained about old Mrs Bromley.'

Andrew nodded. He glanced across at Danny, and the boy stared back, his eyes as cold as stone. Andrew looked quickly away. He wanted to go home. How soon could he get up and leave? He didn't like the Sharmans. He didn't like the house. And besides, he still had some maths to finish. Perhaps if he –

'Now then, how about a drink, everybody?' Mrs Sharman said. 'We've a lot to celebrate.'

'Our new home,' Mr Sharman said.

'And *our* new neighbours,' Andrew's mother said, and giggled.

Mrs Sharman bustled out of the room, leaving the door ajar behind her. Andrew shivered, remembering the chill in the hall.

'Come and sit over here if you're in a draught, dear,' his mother said, and then blushed. 'Not that there *are* any draughts here, I'm sure,' she went on nervously, 'but you can never tell with these old houses – '

'It's as draughty as a tomb,' Mr Sharman said cheerfully. 'Bound to be, isn't it? No central heating, no double – '

'No central heating?' Andrew's mother was horrified. 'However will you manage?'

'Don't worry, we'll have it put in before next winter,' Mr Sharman said. 'We certainly don't need it *now*, though, do we?'

'No, we certainly don't,' Andrew's mother said. 'It's been lovely the past few weeks.'

Mrs Sharman reappeared then with a tray of glasses. 'You'll have to excuse the mess,' she said. 'We haven't had time to unpack properly and I've no idea where anything is. All I could find was this bottle of brandy.'

'That'll be lovely,' Andrew's mother said unconvincingly.

'There must be something else,' Mr Sharman said, and got up to go and look.

Andrew peered round the room. It was tall and gloomy, and the Sharmans' bright modern furniture didn't suit it at all. Mrs Sharman must have followed his glance for she suddenly said, 'Awful, isn't it? The room, I mean. Still, it won't take us long to smarten it up. A bit of white emulsion, some new curtains, and you won't know the place.' She looked round and shuddered theatrically. 'I must say, all this brown paint gives me the creeps. And that hideous wallpaper. We'll have *that* off in no time. Or rather, Alan will.' She laughed loudly.

Andrew's father spoke then for the first time. 'You'll have your work cut out,' he said. 'I shouldn't think old Mrs Bromley ever touched the place, by the look of it. Or the garden, come to that.' He peered hopefully at Mrs Sharman. 'Fond of gardening, are you?'

'Lord, no. I hate it,' Carol Sharman said happily. 'We both do. But then I think wild gardens are so much more fun, don't you? We'll probably leave it as it is.'

Andrew's father stared at her in horror. For as long as Andrew could remember, the garden next door had been a constant irritation to his father. But then it wasn't really a garden at all, more a tangled wilderness of knee-high grass and unkempt elder. For years his father had complained bitterly and regularly to old Mrs Bromley about the dilapidated fence that always collapsed in high winds and about the vicious weeds that advanced beneath it to disturb the geometric order of his lawn. But nothing had come of it. Mrs Bromley had ignored him completely. In fact, she had ignored every living soul in the neighbourhood, apart from the several bad-tempered cats who had shared the house with her.

Mr Sharman's head appeared round the door. 'I've found some red wine,' he said. 'Will that do?'

'Only if you've found the corkscrew as well,' Carol Sharman said.

Mr Sharman muttered something under his breath and disappeared from view once more, to the accompaniment of loud laughter from his wife.

'I hope you don't mind my saying so,' Andrew's mother said, 'but you sound rather American.'

'That's because I am,' Carol Sharman said. 'Milwaukee born and bred, God help me. But don't worry, Alan's as English as fish and chips.'

Andrew's mother looked embarrassed. 'Don't be silly, I wasn't worried. What an idea!' She gave a nervous cough and went on quickly, 'Do you ever go back? For holidays, I mean.'

'Every year,' Mrs Sharman said. 'We go back every summer to visit the old folks at home. In fact, it's not long before our next trip. We'll be going over for six glorious weeks as soon as Danny's term ends.'

'But that's the week after next!' Andrew's mother said.

'I know.' Mrs Sharman pulled a rueful face. 'We won't even have time to unpack properly before we go. But that's how things have worked out. And there'll be plenty of time to sort out the house when we get back.'

'You're all going, are you?' Andrew's mother looked as though she couldn't believe her ears.

'All of us. We'll just shut up the house and fly off into the wide blue yonder.'

'So you'll be away for the summer,' Andrew's mother said. 'Lucky you. All *we're* having is a fortnight in Budleigh Salterton.'

Danny made a noise that could have been a cough but probably wasn't, and his mother gave him a sharp look. 'Why don't you and Andy go into the kitchen and get yourselves a Coke or something,' she said. 'You two should get acquainted, anyway. I'm sure you're going to be the best of friends.'

'Andrew,' said Andrew.

Mrs Sharman looked at him blankly. 'What's that, honey?'

'My name's Andrew,' he said stonily. 'Not Andy.'

'Okay then, Andrew. Go get yourself a coke.' She turned away impatiently and smiled at Andrew's mother. 'Now then, tell me all about the other people in the road. I want the lowdown on *all* our new neighbours.'

Andrew rose to his feet and looked across at Danny, who got up and headed towards the door. 'Come on, *Andy*,' he muttered, and Andrew followed him resentfully into the hall.

He stopped dead as the cold wave of fear rose to meet him again. The hall seemed filled with it, a thick dark blanket of dread that chilled him to the bone. Andrew stood where he was for a moment, paralysed with fright. Yet the hall looked harmless enough. A front door with two panes of decorative stained glass. Some unpacked tea chests piled against the wall. A wide uncarpeted staircase rising to the upper floor. Under the stairs, a cupboard. Andrew noticed that the door was ajar but all he could see inside was darkness. He walked slowly down the hall towards the kitchen, each step bringing him closer to the cupboard. And, as he walked, the fear grew stronger and he knew that something was there. There was something in the cupboard. The fear was coming from the cupboard and he knew that he had to get away from it. He had to get away, quickly. If he didn't –

'Are you coming or aren't you?'

Andrew looked away from the cupboard and saw Danny staring at him, a puzzled frown on his face.

'The kitchen's this way,' the boy said. 'That is, if you *want* a Coke or something.'

'C-coming,' Andrew stammered, and moved towards him. The fear was pressing tightly round him now, dragging him towards the cupboard. He had to get away. He *had* to. And yet – and yet he needed to know if anything was there. He needed to know why he felt so afraid.

Andrew swallowed hard and walked firmly away from the cupboard and into the kitchen. Like the sitting room, it was dark and gloomy, and smelt faintly of gas. Danny was peering into an enormous white refrigerator that looked strangely out of place in the grubby room. He turned round when Andrew came in and handed him a can.

'Here,' he said, then, 'What got into you out there?'

'What do you mean?' Andrew said quickly.

'You looked – you looked sort of weird. When you were in the hall. As if you were frightened of something.'

Andrew smiled nervously. 'Did I? You must be imagining things.'

Danny took a mouthful of Coke. 'Maybe I am. This house gives me the creeps, anyway. I wish we'd stayed in London.'

'Why did you move here?'

'We had to. We move around a lot.' Danny gazed round the room. 'It wouldn't be so bad if we'd found a decent house. A modern one, like yours. This place is a dump. It stinks.'

'An old lady lived here for years,' Andrew said. 'Mrs Bromley. She was mad, I think. She never went out.'

'The house stinks,' Danny said again. 'I hate it.' He drained his can and banged it down on the table. 'Come on, *Andy*, let's get back to the others. It's cold out here.'

Andrew put down his can and caught hold of Danny's arm as he passed. 'We'd better get one thing straight right away,' he said. 'Call me Andy again and I'll knock your teeth right down your stupid throat.'

Danny stared at him, his eyes like pale cold stones. 'Just you try it,' he said at last. 'Just you try.'

He pushed past Andrew and headed for the door.
Andrew waited a moment and then followed him into
the hall. As he did so, the fear rose to meet him once
again, and with it the certainty that something terrible
was hidden behind the door under the stairs. He wanted
to get away from it, he wanted to get as far away as
possible. But first he needed to find out if anything was
there. He had to look inside the cupboard.

By now Danny had reached the sitting room door.
He turned to look back at Andrew and then opened it
and went inside. Andrew stayed where he was, his eyes
fixed on the cupboard under the stairs, on the thin sliver
of darkness revealed by the partly open door.

He took a step towards the cupboard and then
stopped in fright as a sound came from inside it. It was
a low, muffled noise, like someone sobbing. Or choking.
He stood still for a moment and listened. The house was
silent, apart from the murmur of voices from the sitting
room. Surely he'd imagined it? He'd imagined the
sound because he was afraid in the house. There hadn't
been a noise at all. Or, if there had, it was just a floor-
board creaking or something wrong with the plumbing.
There must be noises all the time in an old house like
this. There couldn't possibly –

Then Andrew heard it again. He heard someone
crying. There was someone in the cupboard. There was
someone crying in the darkness under the stairs. Someone who was afraid, someone who needed his help. He
had to find out who was there.

He moved closer and then gasped as a dark wave of
panic washed over him and the noise grew louder. He
lifted a hand to pull the door open and, as he did so,
the sobbing stopped and he could hear words, a voice
in the darkness that moaned, 'Help me! Help me,
please, oh help me, help – '

Andrew pulled open the heavy wooden door and stared into the cupboard. But the darkness was too intense; he could see nothing but blackness, and all he could hear was the drumming of his own heart and a sobbing voice pleading weakly for help. He looked desperately round for a light switch, for anything that might help him to see more clearly, but there was nothing. Only the terrified voice, and the darkness . . .

'Andrew, what on earth are you doing?'

He swung round in fright. Mr Sharman was standing behind him, an empty wine bottle in his hand. 'What on earth are you doing in there?' he repeated.

Andrew blinked at him, struggling desperately for words that wouldn't sound too stupid. 'I – I thought I heard something,' he said lamely.

'Heard something? What sort of something?'

'A – a cat,' Andrew stammered. 'Yes, that's right, I thought your cat was in the cupboard. I thought it was trapped in there, so I – '

'But we haven't got a cat,' Mr Sharman said.

'Oh. Well then, it must have been something else.'

Mr Sharman laughed, and gave him a push in the direction of the sitting room. 'This house is full of noises,' he said. 'Some nights the plumbing sounds like a third-rate orchestra tuning up.'

'Yes,' said Andrew. 'I except it was the plumbing.' He paused when he reached the sitting room door. 'Are you *sure* you haven't got a cat? Or a dog?'

'Quite sure,' smiled Mr Sharman. He turned towards the kitchen and then stopped to look back at Andrew. 'I'd be careful of that cupboard, if I were you.'

Andrew's stomach gave a sudden lurch. 'What do you mean?' he asked.

'I nearly got locked inside it the other day,' Mr Sharman said. 'I was stacking some boxes in there and a draught blew the door shut. You can't open it from the inside.'

'Don't worry, Mr Sharman,' Andrew said. 'I'll stay well clear of it, believe me.' And he opened the sitting room door and rejoined the others.

Andrew couldn't get to sleep that night. Whenever he closed his eyes, he saw again the hall of the Sharmans' house, and the cupboard under the stairs. And, try as he might, he couldn't forget the sound of that desperate pleading voice: 'Help me! Help me, please, oh help me, help – ' It seemed as though the voice was calling to him still, across the few yards of darkness that separated his bedroom from the house next door. He had to go back to the cupboard. He had to find out who was there. They needed his help so badly . . .

He got out of bed and padded in his bare feet to the window. Below lay his father's garden, the neat paths and borders etched by moonlight. To the right, on the other side of the ramshackle fence, lay the Sharmans' garden, dense, tangled and mysterious. Andrew opened the window and leaned out, craning his neck to see the house next door. But all he could manage was a glimpse of a bay window and some insecure guttering. He closed the window and shivered, despite the warmth of the summer night. The fear was with him still, the fear that was echoed in the pitiful voice that he couldn't forget: 'Help me! Help me, please, oh help me, help – '

Andrew got back into bed and buried his head beneath the duvet, trying to shut out the voice. But he couldn't stifle the sound, he couldn't ignore that terrified plea for help. He had to go back. He *had* to.

For he knew that there was something else about that voice, something he'd only dimly realised till now. He had heard the voice before. Somewhere, somehow, he had heard the voice before. He knew who it was. But, try as he might, he couldn't remember. He couldn't for the life of him remember.

It was a week before Andrew was able to return to the house next door. A few days after their first visit, Andrew's mother had insisted on inviting the family over for supper, together with the Parkers from the other side and the Gibsons from across the road. 'The best possible way for the Sharmans to get to know the neighbours,' she'd said. 'Now, I wonder if they'd all like a nice curry? Or maybe it'd better be something more simple, just to be on the safe side.' In the end, she'd decided on an elaborate chicken recipe she'd discovered in a magazine at the dentist's. Andrew hadn't enjoyed the evening at all; he'd been forced to entertain Danny Sharman and the Parker twins, an enterprise complicated by the fact that Danny and the Parkers had taken an instant dislike to each other.

Since then, Andrew had seen quite a bit of the Sharmans in one way or another, either across the garden fence or in the road outside or by chance at the shops. It was a couple of days after the supper party that he'd met Carol Sharman outside the public library, one evening after school.

'Hullo, And – er – Andrew,' she'd said cheerfully. 'Only a few days to go now.' Seeing his blank look, she'd explained, 'We're off to the States next Saturday. There's so much to do . . . ' She looked at Andrew seriously for a moment and went on, 'You know, you're always welcome to come in and see Danny any time you like. The door's always open, so don't wait for an invitation. We never bother to lock our doors, anyway. I always say that if a burglar wants to get in, a locked door isn't going to stop him.' She laughed, and added, 'So don't be such a stranger, Andrew,' before dashing away in the direction of the car park.

Andrew watched her go, his heart pounding. Ever since his visit to the Sharmans, he'd been tormented by the memory of the pleading voice he'd heard that night. He didn't really want to see the Sharmans again. He certainly didn't want to see Danny. But perhaps this would be his chance to find out if he'd only imagined those desperate words, the cold clenching fear.

That evening after supper, Andrew slipped through a gap in the fence that separated the gardens and walked through the long dry grass to the Sharmans' back door. 'The door's always open,' Mrs Sharman had said. He decided to take her at her word. He turned the handle gently and pushed the door open. He stood on the step for a moment and listened. The kitchen beyond seemed to be empty and he stepped carefully inside. He stopped again to listen, and then he walked quickly across the room to the door that led into the hall. It was open.

Andrew could hear the muffled sounds of a television set in the sitting room, and loud music somewhere upstairs. And then, as he stared at the closed cupboard door, these noises faded in his ears, to be replaced by the sound of low sobbing and then the despairing words he knew so well: 'Help me! Help me, please, oh help me, help – '

He crossed to the cupboard and turned the handle. The door swung slowly outwards, releasing a sudden icy blast of fear that made him gasp out loud. He staggered a little, and then took a deep breath, trying to ignore the pounding in his chest and the sobbing words in his ears. He had to find out. He had to help. He had to –

The sitting room door opened and Danny Sharman came into the hall. He stopped short when he saw Andrew, and his eyes widened in surprise. 'What are *you* doing here?' he snapped.

Andrew gaped at him, tense with fear and frustration. 'I – I came to – to see you, I suppose,' he stammered. The voice moaned in his ears still, pleading, imploring.

Danny walked towards him, his gaze cold and scornful. 'Well, I don't want to see *you*,' he said. 'You're a real weirdo, *Andy*. You make me want to throw up.'

Andrew stared at him for a moment and then he leaped at Danny and dragged him to the floor. And it was there that Carol Sharman found them a moment or two later, rolling and punching and kicking and shouting in a frenzy of hatred.

Andrew didn't see any of the Sharmans until the following Saturday morning. He and his parents were sitting in the kitchen having breakfast when there was a knock at the back door and Carol Sharman burst in. She was looking hurried and flustered but accepted the offer of a cup of coffee and sat down at the table to drink it.

'I can't stay long,' she said. 'I've really just called in to say goodbye. We're off to the States today.'

'We're going to miss you,' Andrew's mother said.

Mrs Sharman beamed at her. 'How sweet of you to say so. And we're going to miss all of *you*.' She caught Andrew's eye then and looked quickly away. Nothing had been said to Andrew's parents about his fight with Danny but Mrs Sharman had made it very clear that he was no longer welcome in their house.

'I must say, time does fly,' Andrew's mother said. 'It seems only yesterday that you moved in.'

'It was, dear, it was,' Mrs Sharman laughed. 'But

we're only going away on vacation. We'll back in six weeks. And then we'll *really* have time to get to know each other.' She patted his mother's hand and stood up. 'Now I *must* go. The cab's coming at eleven and we *still* haven't finished packing.'

Andrew stared at her, his mind racing. There wasn't much time left. In two hours the Sharmans would be gone and he wouldn't be able to get into the house. But he *had* to get back inside, he had to find out about the cupboard. There was someone there, someone in trouble. He was sure of it now. Someone needed his help in that fearful darkness. He *had* to get back . . .

His parents were standing up now. 'We'll keep an eye on the house for you,' Andrew's father was saying.

'Bless you!' Carol Sharman said. 'But there's nothing to do. No plants to water, no animals to feed, nothing. We'll just lock the place up and go. Mind you,' and she grinned at him roguishly, 'you might phone the police if you see anyone climbing in but, otherwise, there's no need for you to do anything at all.' And then she was gone, as suddenly as she'd arrived.

Andrew's parents sat down at the table again. 'Pleasant woman,' his mother said. 'For an American.'

'I do wish they'd do something about the garden,' his father said gloomily.

'Never mind, dear. You can't have everything. Let's just be glad we've got some nice neighbours at last.'

Andrew said nothing. He stood up, took his plate to the sink, and then headed for the door.

'And what have *you* got planned for today, young man?' his mother asked.

He paused. 'Nothing much,' he mumbled. 'I've got an essay to finish for Monday. Then I thought I might go into town for a bit. Or over to Pete Millard's place. I don't know.'

'Well, don't forget lunch is at one sharp.'

'No, I won't,' he said.

Andrew knew exactly what to do. He went up to his bedroom and worked on his essay about Martin Luther and the Reformation until half past ten. Then he came quietly downstairs and peered into the kitchen. It was empty. He slipped out of the back door and into the garden. His father was busy in the greenhouse at the far end but he had his back to the house and so he didn't see Andrew squeezing through a gap in the fence into the garden next door.

He paused on the other side to get his breath and then ran through the tangled grass until he reached the back door of the Sharmans' house. There was no sound inside and so he turned the handle gently, praying that the door hadn't been locked. His luck was in. The door opened quietly and he peered inside. There was no one in the kitchen. He crossed to the half-open door that led to the hall and stood for a moment, listening. There was the sound of loud voices on the floor above and then Mr Sharman staggered down the stairs, carrying two large suitcases. He stacked them by the front door and then climbed the stairs again.

When he had gone, Andrew crept out of the kitchen and crossed the hall to the cupboard under the stairs. He opened the door, bracing himself for the rush of panic that he knew would meet him, waiting for the terrified voice pleading for help. But this time there was nothing. He felt no rush of fear and heard no voice. All he could see was darkness.

And then he heard footsteps on the staircase above and he darted into the cupboard, pulling the door to behind him until only a sliver of light remained. He could hear voices in the hall now but he could see nothing, just the wall opposite the door.

'Is that everything now?' Carol Sharman said.

'I think so.' Her husband sounded tired and irritable. 'If you've forgotten anything we'll just have to buy another one when we get there. Everything packed, Danny?'

'Yes,' Danny said.

'The taxi will be here any minute,' Mr Sharman said. 'I'll go round and lock up.'

'I'll check upstairs,' Danny said, and Andrew flinched as the boy's footsteps thundered over his head. Then he ducked instinctively as Mr Sharman walked past the cupboard into the kitchen. He heard the back door being locked.

'The cab's here!' Mrs Sharman called.

Mr Sharman came out of the kitchen, and then Andrew heard Danny's footsteps on the stairs above. There was the sound of the front door opening, of cases being carried outside and loaded into a car. Then the sound of returning footsteps.

'Is that everything?' Mr Sharman said. 'Are we all set?'

'I think so,' said his wife. 'Oh Danny, just shut that cupboard, will you?'

'Sure,' said Danny.

Andrew heard approaching footsteps. He opened his mouth to shout but no words came and the cupboard door slammed shut like thunder. He heard more footsteps then, and the sound of muffled voices. And after that, the final slam of the front door.

Andrew sat alone in the darkness under the stairs. The house was now completely silent. It was then that the fear returned at last, the blind desperate panic that he knew so well. He shouted as loudly as he could but he knew that there was no one to hear his cries. He could see nothing at all in the darkness and all he could hear was the thunderous pounding of his heart and the sound of someone sobbing: 'Help me! Help me, please, oh help me, help – '

And he knew then why the voice seemed so familiar. It was his own.

The Sea Bride

Vivien Alcock

Vivien Alcock

The Sea Bride

The moment I saw her, I wanted her. She was standing on the pavement outside Willoughby's, staring over my head with her bold black eyes. Nothing warned me. No cloud suddenly darkened the sky. No wind blew coldly down my neck. I thought she was beautiful.

My father and I are hunters. Bargain hunters. Walter Muffat, Antiques, that's us. Or rather, that's my father. When I'm grown up, I'm going to be '& SON' in gold letters over our shop. At the moment, I'm only Sam Muffat, Oddments.

During the school holidays, I have a stall in the paved yard beside our shop. A hand-painted notice says: SAM MUFFAT. ODDMENTS. BARGAINS. IF YOU CAN'T AFFORD ANYTHING INSIDE, TRY ME.

My mother disapproved. She said it looked cheap. But my father just laughed.

'Everyone has to begin small,' he said. 'Sam's doing all right. You can't start too young at this game.'

For I was only twelve, just twelve; it was my birthday. I felt rich and lucky, setting out for Willoughby's Sale Rooms with my father. I had thirty-eight pounds in my pocket, part birthday money and part savings, and I was going to buy the bargain that would make my fortune. Or so I thought.

But Willoughby's was far grander than the local auctions I was used to. Far grander than the sales, (jumble and church bazaar) where I normally bought things for my stall. It was crowded with dealers from London, who nodded to my father, glanced at me briefly, and then talked above my head as if I was not there. I wanted to tell them that I was a dealer like themselves, but I seemed to have lost my voice.

There were not enough chairs and, being only a boy, I did not get one. I perched on the edge of a table, (Victorian, mahogany, one leg repaired) until a porter shooed me off. Then I sat on a window-sill so sharp and narrow that I feared it would slice me in two. As I watched and listened, the money in my pocket seemed to shrivel. My father had warned me. 'Thirty-eight pounds won't go far at Willoughby's,' he'd said. He was right.

'Who'll start me at a hundred?' the auctioneer asked. 'I'm offered a hundred. A hundred and ten. A hundred and twenty. A hundred and forty. Any advance on a hundred and forty?'

I began to think I'd never get a chance to make a bid.

Then one of the porters held up a china shepherdess, complete with sheep. (Staffordshire, circa 1875)

'What am I bid for this? Who'll start me at twenty pounds?'

I still could not find my voice, but that didn't worry me. Many dealers just signal to the auctioneer by raising their catalogues or nodding their heads. There is a joke that if you sneeze at an auction, you may find you have bought a grand piano by mistake. It isn't true. I could have had hay fever and the auctioneer wouldn't have cared. He saw me raise my catalogue. I know he did! He looked straight at me. His glance travelled from my head to my toes and back again, (not a long journey: I'm small for my age). Then he ignored me and took the bid from a fat women in a green coat.

'Twenty pounds I'm bid. Twenty-two. Twenty-four. Twenty-six. Any advance on twenty-six?'

This time I waved my catalogue so vigorously that I nearly fell off the window-sill. He noticed me then all right.

'I'm not sure if the young gentleman over there is bidding,' he said. 'Or swatting a fly.'

Everyone laughed and turned to look at me. My face went crimson. I hated them. I mumbled something inaudible, slid off the window-sill and tried, unsuccessfully, to sink through the floor.

'My son was bidding,' my father said, annoyed on my behalf. 'Twenty-eight pounds you're bid, sir.'

The fat woman in the green coat smiled at me nastily.

'Thirty,' she said.

It went for thirty-six pounds, and not to me. I didn't want it any longer. I didn't want anything in that beastly sale room. I was no longer certain I wanted to be '& SON' in gold letters over our shop door.

My father glanced at me, worried that I was disappointed with my birthday treat. He is a very nice man, my father. So I smiled at him and whispered, 'Well, I broke the ice, didn't I? Talking of ice, I think I'll pop out for a lolly. Back in half-an-hour.' I waved my hand jauntily, trying not to look like someone who'd had his first bid ignored and his second made fun of.

So that is how I came to be outside Willoughby's, cooling my hot cheeks in the fresh air, when they unloaded her from the van and placed her carefully on the pavement. For my black-eyed beauty was a ship's figurehead. She was leaning forward as if breasting the waves. Her hair, black and glossy with paint, streamed back over her shoulders. Her cheeks were pink, her skin white, and her breasts, big as water melons, seemed about to burst out of her sea-green dress. She had, of course, no feet. A heavy iron stand supported her, otherwise she'd have fallen flat on her nose.

They could keep their simpering china shepherdesses. I wanted this stern beauty, (for she was not smiling). Her black eyes, fixed so intently on a faraway horizon, seemed to reflect wonders I could not see; strange islands, flying fish, great white whales . . . She had about her the very smell of the sea, and glistened in her bright paint as if still wet. A shop awning, flapping in the breeze, sounded like a galleon in full sail. The paving stones seemed to tilt beneath my feet, as if the town was suddenly afloat. I wanted her. I wanted her in our yard, between my stall and the tub of scarlet geraniums, attracting the eye of every rich customer who strolled by. But I did not think I could afford her.

The dealer who owned her, (H Wiggins & Son it said on the side of his van) was arguing with one of the porters from Willoughby's.

'We can't possibly get her in before the 17th, sir,' the porter was saying.

'That's no good. Today. It must be today. Surely you can slip her in at the end . . . '

'I'm sorry, sir. We're running late as it is,' the porter said.

'I could make it worth your while,' the man suggested, clinking some money in his pocket. But the porter was not interested. I knew him. His name was Alf and he had a girl-friend who worked in Boots. Perhaps he was taking her out that night. Perhaps it was *his* birthday.

'We can store her for you, sir,' he suggested.

H Wiggins looked doubtful.

'I'm going away today. I wanted to be rid . . . I wanted her off my hands.'

As they talked, I was walking round my beauty, examining her with a connoisseur's eye. The paint, which had looked fresh and new from a distance, now revealed cracks through which you could see the wood. It was old, but sound. Oak, I thought, very dark; weathered. I put my hand out . . .

'Don't touch!' said a young man sharply. He had been leaning against the van, a thin figure in faded jeans and a tattered jersey – '& Son', I thought.

'He's trade,' Alf said, nodding towards me, 'Walter Muffat, Antiques. Son of. Perhaps you can do a private deal.' He winked at me and hurried back into the auction rooms.

H Wiggins & Son looked at me thoughtfully.

'Trade, eh?' said the older man, 'Is your dad inside?' He jerked his thumb towards Willoughby's.

I shook my head. It wasn't really a lie. I mean, I didn't actually say 'no'. I was just shaking the hair out of my eyes. I couldn't help it if they misunderstood me.

'I might be interested, if the price is right,' I said. 'I'm a dealer.'

I waited for them to laugh; people usually do when I say this, but not H Wiggins & Son. If anything, they looked sad. Their faces were pale and weary. Their dark eyes surveyed me seriously, with a kind of gloomy hope.

I suppose it should have warned me, but I was enjoying myself at last. I strutted round the figurehead, peered closely at the paint, ran my fingers lightly down her arm, rapped her with my knuckles, as if by doing so, I could immediately tell if she were wormy or cracked.

'Sound as a bell,' the older man said.

'She's been repainted,' I said sternly, for the paint, though cracked, could not have been the original.

'Restored,' he countered.

'Hmm-mm,' I stroked my chin with my thumb, just as my father did when he was pretending to be doubtful.

'Where's she from?' I asked next.

'Newcastle. Off a Victorian frigate. *The Sea Bride*, it was – sailed the East India run in her day. *The Sea Bride*, now there's a pretty name for her.' He raised his hand as if to slap her bottom, but thought better of it and put his hand in his pocket. 'And a right buxom beauty she is too,' he said, staring at her.

His expression puzzled me. There was no admiration in it; whatever he might say. He looked almost as if he hated her. But I, with thirty-eight pounds in my pocket, and my head filled with sailing-ships on bright seas, heard no warning bell.

'What are you asking for her?' I said.

They closed in, one on either side of me. I felt very small between them.

'Make me an offer,' H Wiggins said.

I did not want to. I was afraid they would laugh when they heard how little I had to give. For I thought she was worth at least two hundred pounds.

I stepped back. Shrugged. Shook my head slowly. They watched me.

'Business is bad,' I said.

And they nodded, almost eagerly.

'People are not buying, not things like this,' I gestured at the figurehead.

Now they were shaking their heads. 'No. Things are very slow,' they agreed. 'Money's tight. You'd not find a buyer easily for her.'

I was disconcerted. They seemed to be on my side. This was not the way bargaining was usually done.

'Come on, young sir,' the father said, 'for a quick sale, I'm prepared to let her go cheap. Dirt cheap. Don't be shy. Make me an offer. I'll not laugh, however small it is.'

'Twenty-five pounds,' I said, and my voice squeaked with embarrassment.

But they did not laugh. They exchanged unreadable glances.

Then the father said, 'Fifty.'

I was astonished. Only fifty pounds? My heart began to race. I tried not to look excited, but I could feel my cheeks flushing.

'Thirty,' I said.

'Oh, you're in luck, young sir. I'm in a generous mood today. Forty pounds – and not a penny less.'

So near. So nearly mine.

'Thirty-five.' Now my voice was hoarse, 'thirty-five – and not a penny more.'

'*Done!*' H Wiggins spoke so quickly that his mouth opened and shut like a trap. 'It's a bargain.'

He held out his hand and I shook it. Then, finding he was still holding it out, I counted the money into it with shaking fingers. He gave me a receipt, stuffed the money carelessly into his pocket, and smiled for the first time.

'You drive a hard bargain, son of Walter Muffat, Antiques,' he said. 'You're too sharp for an old fellow like me. She's yours, young sir. Not mine any longer. All yours.' His eyes now seemed full of a secret glee. 'And may you have better luck with her than I had.'

He climbed into his van. I heard the engine start.

His son still lingered on the pavement. He looked ill. His eyes, in his thin face, were reddened, with dark smudges under them, as if he had not slept for many nights.

He came up close to me and said in a low voice, 'Keep her out of doors. Don't bring her into the shop. Don't let her into the house.'

I must have looked surprised because he added quickly, 'She'll come to no harm. Not her. Rain and sleet, hail and wind, they'll not hurt *her*. Leave her outside, and . . .' here his voice sank to a whisper, 'and shut your windows at night.'

Then he too jumped into the van, and it disappeared down the street in a cloud of exhaust. I stood on the pavement, staring after them in astonishment. My father, coming out of Willoughby's to look for me, laughed when he saw me there. He said I looked bewitched. He said I was rocking on my feet, as if I were all at sea.

We put the Sea Bride in the yard, beside the tub of scarlet geraniums. I wished the sun had not gone in. I wanted her to look her best.

'I don't like her,' my sister said. Becky is only seven, and very silly.

But my mother was impressed.

'Thirty-five pounds!' she exclaimed. 'You're joking! There must be something wrong.' (This is high praise from my mother. She never trusts bargains if they seem too good. Dad says that when he offered her his hand and heart, she examined them under a magnifying glass for hidden flaws.) 'Did he give you a receipt?'

'Yes.' I handed it to her.

'H Wiggins & Son, Portsmouth. Never heard of them. Have you, Walter?'

My father shook his head. 'Lots of dealers I haven't heard of,' he said cheerfully. But he too looked puzzled. 'What was the man thinking of? He could have got a couple of hundred for her in any sale room.'

'Perhaps he didn't like her,' Becky said. 'Perhaps he didn't like the way she stares.'

'Do you think she's a fake, Dad?' I asked anxiously.

'She looks genuine enough to me. Not that I'm an expert. Not my line. I'll get old Watson to have a look at her. Don't worry, Sam. She's well worth the money, even if they knocked her up in their own back yard. She's a handsome lass. The Sea Bride, eh? Mrs Neptune herself. I hope her old man doesn't come and fetch her away.'

'What old man?' Becky asked.

'Father Neptune,' I explained. You always have to explain jokes to Becky.

'Who's he?'

'The sea god.'

'Why'd he want her?'

'She's his bride. The Sea Bride, see?'

'The She Bride?'

Becky could go on like this for hours.

'Oh, shut up!' I said.

'Your Mrs Neptune's a haughty young madam, isn't she?' my mother said. 'Looks as if she didn't think our yard was good enough for her.'

'Don't you like her, Mum?'

'Oh, . . . yes. Yes, dear, of course,' she said doubtfully.

'I don't! She's horrible!' Becky said. 'I hate her!'

What was the matter with them? Then I thought, catching sight of a smudge of chocolate icing on Becky's cheek, it's my birthday. That's the trouble. Other people's birthdays go on too long.

I took pity on them. 'What's for tea?' I asked.

Becky beamed happily.

'Sea biscuits and salt water! Sea biscuits and salt water!' she chanted shrilly, and shrieked with laughter.

Funny. We are thirty miles or more from the nearest coast, yet I fancied, for a moment, that I could smell salt water. And I did not want to go into the house and eat sausages and peanuts, sandwiches and candled cake. I wanted to stay in the yard, where the cool breeze seemed to carry the tang of the faraway sea. I glanced back. She looked lonely, my black-eyed beauty. Leaning forward, she strained against her iron stand, as if she wanted to get away.

There was a high wind in the night. Though I slept through it, its wailing must have invaded my dreams. I had a nightmare, but I cannot remember what it was about. I woke, carrying only the terror with me from my sleep. Becky was in my room.

'Sam! Wake up, Sam!' she cried. 'Your Mrs Neptune's got away!'

I leapt out of bed and ran to the window. In the yard below, there were broken tiles on the paving-stones. The dustbins had blown over and scattered their rubbish everywhere. A branch had broken off the silver birch. Then I saw her. She had fallen across our wrought-iron gates and was leaning out into the street.

'Sam!' called my father, catching sight of me at the window. 'Come and help!'

'How did she get there?'

'Dunno. Must have blown, I suppose. Funny. You'd have thought she'd have fallen over before she reached the gate. Lucky we shut them at night or there's no telling where she'd have gone.'

She was heavy and part of her stand had got caught in one of the decorative loops of the gates. My father could not lift her by himself. I dressed quickly and went to help him. Seen so close, her eyes were as black and shiny as tar. She gazed down the hill so eagerly; it was hard to believe she wasn't looking at something, something too far away for me to see. It wasn't the road to the coast. That was at the back of our house.

'If you went on and on that way, as far as you could,' I said, pointing, 'where would you get to, Dad?'

'Ease her back a little, Sam. A bit more,' my father said. 'Steady now. Up she rises . . .'

She was heavy. 'Dad,' I panted, 'where would you get to, if . . . '

'I heard you the first time. (Steady now! Careful does it!) Why, I suppose you'd come to the sea in the end. We're on an island. Whichever way you go, you'd come to the sea in the end.'

My poor Sea Bride. That afternoon, my father bolted her iron stand to the wall behind her.

'We don't want her running off again,' he said. 'That should hold her.'

I thought she looked angry. I swept and tidied our yard, and weeded the tubs of scarlet geraniums. If I thought to appease her, it did not work. That night, water somehow got into our shop, staining the polished top of a Sheraton table and soaking the set of tapestry chairs.

'Where's it come from?' my father demanded angrily. He looked upwards, almost as if he were reproaching God. There were no damp patches on the ceiling.

'Did you leave a window open?' my mother asked.

'Of course not!'

'Perhaps it came down the chimney,' I suggested.

'Don't be so stupid, Sam!' he shouted.

I flushed and went out, ignoring the apology he called after me. Becky followed me into the yard.

'It's her,' she whispered. '*She* did it.'

'Don't be so stupid,' I said, thinking I might as well pass it on.

'She did! She did! She's a sea witch!' Becky said. 'I hate her!'

She stood in front of Mrs Neptune and put out her tongue. Then suddenly she looked scared. She ran over to me and took hold of my hand. She really is very silly at times.

'She can't hurt you,' I said comfortingly. I reached out and tapped the white wooden arm: 'She's not real.'

'Touch wood! You're touching wood!' Becky cried, and giggled.

The Sea Bride stared over our heads with her bold black eyes. The sun came out, and a small wind stirred in the ivy. Again I seemed to smell the salt tang of the sea, as if it were a perfume she wore.

'Who's she looking for?' Becky whispered. 'Who does she keep looking for?'

I woke early next morning. It must have poured in the night. I had not shut my window and the curtains were soaked. There was a dark, wet stain on the carpet like blood. The dye had run from my new slippers; when I picked them up, my hands were red.

I stared out of the window. In the yard below, Mrs Neptune stood, glittering wet in the morning light. How beautiful she looked. Almost alive. I could have sworn a strand of her hair moved gently in the wind.

I dressed quickly and went outside. Puddles of water lay in the hollows of the paving; and little stones, grey and brown, were scattered everywhere. As I walked, I looked round, puzzled. Then I stepped on something soft and fleshy, like a fat man's hand. I snatched my foot back.

It was a fish, dead; its round eye glazed, its silver skin striped with black. A mackerel.

I picked it up. It was quite stiff. At first I thought

our cat had been raiding the larder. Then I noticed there were more of them, floating in puddles, caught up in the ivy, half-hidden among the red geraniums. There must have been twenty, at least.

I gathered them into an old bucket and hid them in the shed. I don't know why. They made me uneasy, somehow. Then I swept up the shingle and hid it behind the dustbins. My mother came out as I was putting the broom away.

'You're up early, Sam. Tidying up again for Mrs Neptune, I see. Well, she doesn't seem to have suffered in the storm last night.'

'Rain and sleet, hail and wind, they won't hurt *her*,' I said.

Mum looked surprised. 'Is that from a poem?' she asked. 'Well, she may be weatherproof, but if you ask me, it was just as well Dad bolted her stand to the wall. She might have fallen over and cracked. Breakfast in ten minutes, Sam.'

'It's not mackerel, is it, Mum?'

'No. Why, did you fancy one? I could get one for your tea, if you like.'

'No. I don't like fish.'

She looked at me, then shook her head, smiling. 'Kids!' she said, and went back into the house.

I went into the shed, took the fish out of the bucket and wrapped them in an old piece of sacking. Then I went out through the yard gate, walked quickly down the street and put my bundle into old Mrs Rutherford's dustbin, pushing it well down till it was hidden beneath the eggshells and tea leaves.

On my way back, running through our yard, I slipped on something and fell, grazing the skin off my knees. A piece of weed had brought me down. I peeled it off my sandal. Dark brown it was, and rubbery, covered with little blisters that popped between my fingers. Seaweed. It stank of the sea. How did it get there? How did the fish and shingle get there? I did not know. We are thirty miles from the nearest coast.

'Why are you lying down?' It was my sister, still in her nightgown, her bare feet paddling in a puddle. 'Did she knock you over?'

'Who?'

'Her. Mrs Neptune.'

'Don't be silly,' I said, picking myself up. 'She's not real. She's only made of wood.

Becky said nothing. She was sucking the sleeve of her nightie, and looking sly.

'Why don't you like her?' I asked curiously.

At first I thought she was not going to tell me. Then she came over, caught hold of my ear and pulled my head down to her level. 'She doesn't like you,' she whispered.

I was hurt. It's silly, I know, but somehow it hurt me. I looked at Mrs Neptune. I still thought she was beautiful. As ever, her black eyes stared over my head. Leaning forward on her stand, she looked eager, expectant, as if she were waiting for someone. But not for me.

That night I shut my window. My mother, coming into my room to kiss me goodnight, complained that it was like an oven.

'Why have you shut your window, Sam? You'll never sleep in this heat.'

'Don't open it, Mum! Leave it! Please.'

She looked at me in surprise.

'It's going to rain tonight,' I said.

'A little rain won't hurt. Better than baking.' She

opened the window about six inches from the top. 'There,' she said.

As soon as she had gone downstairs, I shut it again. Then I tiptoed into Becky's room next door. She was asleep, clutching her teddy bear. Gently, slowly, I closed her window. She did not stir.

When I woke up, it was dark. My bed was rocking. Water crashed against the window. Wind screamed down the chimney. The whole house shuddered and swayed about me. Something crashed downstairs. My light would not work.

I heard my sister scream. Footsteps ran along the passage to her room. I heard my mother's voice.

I was out of bed. I crossed the heaving floor to the window and looked out. It was all black and banging outside. Then lightning lit the sky. Down below, I saw the Sea Bride. White birds screamed about her head. She was leaning into the wind and the waves. She looked huge, alive, triumphant. Great grey mountains of water swirled about her. I saw some dark wood smash against the wall of our house. A piece of wrecked ship? Our garden bench? I did not know. It was all dark again.

I leaned against the window-sill and felt it crack and quiver. I heard my father shout downstairs, and my sister screamed again.

I opened my window wide. Water smashed into my face, soaking me, blinding me, salt on my lips. I clung to the window-sill and screamed into the dark.

'Stop it! Stop it! I'll let her go! I promise! I'll let her go!'

There must have been another flash of lightning. I saw a huge, green, translucent wave coming for me. I thought it had a face. Dark whirlpools were its eyes, wild hair and beard like a waterfall streamed over its cheeks and chin. Then the water held me, shook me, curled round me and tried to suck me out into the wild night. My fingers scrabbled at the window-sill – and slipped.

Now my father's arms were round me. He threw me across the room on to my bed and slammed the window shut.

'Tell him I'll give her back!' I screamed. Then I must have fainted.

'Terrible storm, wasn't it?' my mother said.

It was five in the morning. We were sitting on damp chairs in the damp kitchen, drinking tea. Outside, everything was quiet. No-one answered her. We did not know what to say.

The silence seemed to worry her.

Never known anything like it. If you ask me, it's all these atom bombs. It's not natural.'

'No,' said my father. Then he put down his cup and looked at me. 'Better get going. Are you sure you still want to do it, Sam?'

'Yes.'

'Walter, it's silly,' my mother said uneasily, 'throwing away good money.'

'Don't stop them, Mum! Don't! Please don't!' Becky cried, and began to whimper. Mum put her arm round her and was silent.

My father and I went out into the yard. It was littered with debris. Our garden bench was in pieces. Broken tiles were scattered on the wet paving. The geraniums had lost all their petals, which lay like drops of blood among the broken glass.

Only the Sea Bride was undamaged. Bolted to the wall, she still stared over our heads with her round black eyes.

My father had brought out a wrench and a screwdriver. We unfastened her from her iron stand and carried her out to our van. Thirty miles through the quiet, grey morning we drove, until we reached the shore. Even without her stand, she was heavy. We put her on our trolley and dragged it over the shingle to an old wall that ran into the sea like a stone finger. There was no-one about. We wheeled the trolley along the wide flat top of the wall. The sea had been quiet when we came, but now little waves ran out to greet us. They lapped at our feet, like small wet hands hurrying us along.

'Careful, Sam,' my father said. 'It's slippery.'

There were larger waves now. As we neared the end of the wall, we could see them hurrying over the smooth surface of the sea. There was one behind them, a great green mountain, capped with a crest of snow.

'Good God!' my father cried, and grabbed my arm.

But they did not swamp us. Instead they seemed to hold back, rearing up from the body of the sea in peaks of foam.

'Quick!'

We picked up the Sea Bride between us, and threw her into the sea. A wave rushed to meet her, lifted her on high and spun her round. Now she was facing us. White spray dimmed her black hair like a bridal veil. As she sank, her eyes, at last on my level, gazed straight into mine. I thought she smiled. Then the wave spun her round again and carried her swiftly out to sea. We watched until she was a mere speck, skimming the green water.

Points for Discussion and Suggestions for Writing

The Shadow-Cage

1 Discuss why it was that Kevin, who had desperately wanted the bottle, didn't *need* it once he had obtained it.

2 Describe an occasion when you had pestered your parents for something, perhaps when you were much younger, and then when you had got it you realised you no longer wanted it.

3 Consider the reasons why Kevin felt he must find the green bottle again. Was it just because he had promised to give it back to Lisa?

4 How does Whistlers' Hill affect Kevin while he lies in the shadow-cage? Write a poem describing his thoughts and fears as he lies in the playground.

5 In groups, talk about characters you remember from your childhood who you thought might be witches. Remember the way they looked and the places they lived in as well as the things they did which made you suspicious.

6 Imagine you are Ned Challis. Write a conversation between him and his wife about the events of the day and night after he found the bottle. You could make, with a friend, a dramatised tape of the conversation.

On the Brighton Road

7 Consider how the weather has affected the tramp during his sleep. Discuss the ways in which his words 'Am I glad or sorry it was only sleep that took me?' anticipate the events of the rest of this story.

8 Write an account of the meeting between the tramp and the boy from the boy's point of view. You may wish to include some ideas which show that the boy is familiar with death.

9 Draw an atmospheric picture to illustrate this story. You might like to give it a title with suitably sinister lettering.

0 The boy suggests to the tramp that he might already be dead. In small groups, discuss and then write or maybe make a tape about what you all imagine happens after we die. You may like to consider also what has helped you to form these opinions.

If She Bends, She Breaks

1 In this story, precise descriptions of the places mentioned are very important. Using the evidence given to help you, draw a careful pictorial map of the village, the surrounding countryside and River Pingle, marking the school as well as the exact spot of the accident. Perhaps you could mark some of the children's tracks through the snow.

2 Imagine you are Miss Carter. Write a letter to the Education Authority describing the day's events.

3 Write a newspaper story taking the headline: MYSTERY DEATH ON THIN ICE. Set your work out like a tabloid newspaper, illustrating the story if you

wish. The story itself could be entirely your own, or you could use some of the ideas from this one.

The July Ghost

14 This is a very complicated and disconcerting story where the boundaries between the natural and supernatural worlds are frequently blurred. Because of this, it is important for you to establish the sequence of events before discussing their implications. In groups, make a list of the things which happen to the man which you feel are important. Then consider whether you think the man was foolish to become the woman's lodger. In what ways did he find her strange?

15 What does Noel, the woman's husband, mean when he says: 'You can't throw a life away . . . can you?'?

16 Write a conversation between Noel and a journalist friend of his in a pub, where Noel tries to justify his desire to have assignments away from London in the future.

17 Imagine you are the man in the story. Write a series of diary entries during your stay in the house, including a description of your first encounter with the boy.

18 Discuss whether you think the woman was 'so sensible' when she made Noel destroy all the photographs of their son. In groups, consider the different attitudes you have about how best to overcome grief of this nature.

19 Why do you think the boy 'returns' to his parents' house so frequently, and why might it be that the man can see him whereas his mother cannot?

20 If the woman *had* had another child, do you think it

would have helped her come to terms with her son's death? Consider the reasons for your opinion.

1 Reread the last section of the story from 'He got out his suitcases . . . ' and then talk with a partner about what you understand the passage to mean. Will he be able to leave the house or is he now part of the after-life too?

2 Write a poem entitled 'A Ghost-Child's Return'.

The Red Room

3 Imagine you are the costume-designer for a TV version of this tale. Draw the three old people showing exactly what they would wear and what materials you would use to make their costumes.

4 At the end of the story, the young man explains the ghost by saying: 'The worst of all the things that haunt poor mortal man . . . is, in all its nakedness – *Fear*!' Do you agree with him? Give reasons for your views.

5 Write about a place you have visited or a room you know well that was perfectly 'friendly' by day but became 'fearful' by night. Look at the language used in the story to give you ideas about how to make yours vivid and exciting.

6 The old man says: 'The room will be haunted so long as this house of sin endures'. Imagine that the young man determines to break the curse. Write the story of his attempt; it is up to you to decide whether he is successful or not!

Andrina

7 Consider why Andrina visited Captain Torvald when she did and the reasons she ceased to when she did.

28 What do we know about Captain Torvald by the end of the story? What is your own, as well as a friend's attitude to him?

29 Do you think the last paragraph of the story is rightly optimistic, and if so, why?

30 Imagine you are Torvald. Write a reply to the letter you have just received from Australia.

31 Write the legend of Sigrid, as told by the postmistress, Miss Stewart. It might work well on tape with sound effects suitable to a remote Scottish island.

A Kind of Swan Song

32 Think about the way that everyday detail, such as the exact meal that the mother was preparing for Lisa, builds up the tension of the story. What other effects does it have?

33 Many tragic events happen in this story: the death of a father and of a child. But what is your overall impression of the mood of the story? Discuss your opinions in groups.

34 Can you explain how the tape of Lisa's carol may have been made? Share your ideas with a few friends and then discuss them with the class.

35 Imagine you are one of the policewomen or policemen who had witnessed the accident. Write a conversation in which you tell your husband or wife about the events at Lisa's house, and what you thought you had heard.

The Man Who Didn't Believe in Ghosts

36 Reread the letters and diaries that the laird's son and

the lawyer's daughter wrote. Then imagine you are the daughter's ghost and write a diary of the events up to your final 'release'.

37 Take the title 'I don't believe in ghosts' and write a play where the central character is forced to reconsider his opinion. Then make a taped version with good use of suitable music and other sound effects.

The Darkness under the Stairs

38 Can you imagine what happened next? Write a further episode, revealing whether Andrew escapes or is locked for ever under the stairs.

39 Describe an occasion when you have felt yourself to be locked in. Make your writing as powerful as possible by considering the words you use carefully.

40 In groups, discuss what it is about the Sharmans that makes Andrew and his family feel uncomfortable.

The Sea Bride

41 Describe an occasion when you have desperately wanted something in a shop. Tell the story of that object, seen from its own point of view. What happens when the owner's fascination with it ceases?

42 There are some dramatic descriptions of the storms that beat against the Muffats' house while the Sea Bride is in their yard. Using these as a guide, illustrate a part of the story you particularly enjoyed. Or, write a poem taking 'The Sea Bride' as your title.

43 Write a letter from Sam to his grandparents thanking

them for his birthday money and telling them how he spent it and what happened next.

General questions

44 In groups, consider for what reasons ghosts might appear.

45 Do you think all of us are equally able to see ghosts and to feel the presence of the supernatural, or does this only happen to 'special' people? Using the evidence from these stories, when would ghosts be most likely to appear to us?

46 How do you think writers use the names of the characters and places in their stories to enhance their writing? Choose some examples from this book which you think are succesful.

47 Which of these stories did you find most challenging or disturbing? In answering, try to explain why this was. You will need to write about the plot, the characters and the descriptions.

Wider Reading

Aiken, Joan, *A Touch of Chill* (Fontana)
              A Whisper in the Night (Gollancz)
Alcock, Vivien, *The Stonewalkers* (Fontana)
            Ghostly Companions (Fontana)
Chambers, Aidan, *Book of Ghosts and Hauntings*
         (Puffin)
            Ghost after Ghost (Puffin)
            Shades of Dark (Puffin)
Conan Doyle, Arthur, *The Hound of the Baskervilles*
         (Puffin)
            The Lost World (Puffin)
Cresswell, Helen, *Haunting Short Stories*
         (Octopus)
Garfield, Leon, *The Wedding Ghost* (Oxford)
            Smith (Puffin)
Gordon, John, *House on the Brink* (Puffin)
            Ghost on the Hill (Puffin)
Haining, Peter, (Ed.) *The Ghost Companion* (Puffin)
Hitchcock, Alfred, (Ed.) *Ghostly Gallery* (Puffin)
Ireson, Barbara, (Ed.) *Haunting Tales* (Puffin)
James, Henry, *The Turn of the Screw*
James, M R, *Oh Whistle and I'll Come to You*
Kipling, Rudyard, *They*
Lively, Penelope, *Uninvited Ghosts* (Puffin)
Mackay Brown, George, *Andrina and Other Stories*
         (The Hogarth Press)
Mahy, Margaret, *The Haunting* (Magnet)

Pearce, Philippa, *The Shadow-Cage and Other Tales of the Supernatural* (Puffin)

Tom's Midnight Garden (Puffin)

Salway, Lance, *The Darkness under the Stairs* (Lutterworth Press)

Wells, H G, *Collected Short Stories*

Westall, Robert, *The Scarecrows* (Puffin)

Longman Imprint Books
General Editor: Michael Marland CBE MA

Titles in the series
There is a Happy Land Keith Waterhouse
The Human Element Stan Barstow
Conflicting Generations Five television scripts
*****A Sillitoe Selection** *edited by* Michael Marland
*****Late Night on Watling Street and other stories** Bill Naughton
Black Boy Richard Wright
Scene Scripts Seven television plays
Ten Western Stories *edited by* C E J Smith
Loves, Hopes and Fears *edited by* Michael Marland
Cider with Rosie Laurie Lee
Goalkeepers are Crazy Brian Glanville
A James Joyce Selection *edited by* Richard Adams
Out of the Air Five radio plays *edited by* Alfred Bradley
Scene Scripts Two Five television plays
Caribbean Stories *edited by* Michael Marland
An Isherwood Selection *edited by* Geoffrey Halson
A Thomas Hardy Selection *edited by* Geoffrey Halson
The Experience of Parenthood *edited by* Chris Buckton
The Experience of Love *edited by* Michael Marland
Twelve War Stories *edited by* John L Foster
A Roald Dahl Selection *edited by* Roy Blatchford
A D H Lawrence Selection *edited by* Geoffrey Halson
I'm the King of the Castle Susan Hill
Sliding Leslie Norris
Still Waters Three television plays by Julia Jones
Scene Scripts Three Four television plays *edited by* Roy Blatchford
Television Comedy Scripts Five scripts *edited by* Roy Blatchford
Juliet Bravo Five television scripts
Meetings and Partings Sixteen short stories *compiled by* Michael Marland
Women *compiled and edited by* Maura Healy
Strange Meeting Susan Hill
Looks and Smiles Barry Hines
A Laurie Lee Selection *edited by* Chris Buckton
P'tang, Yang, Kipperbang and other TV plays Jack Rosenthal
Family Circles Five plays *edited by* Alfred Bradley *and* Alison Leake
Humour and Horror Twelve plays *edited by* Caroline Bennitt
Scene Scripts Four Four television plays *edited by* Alison Leake
A Second Roald Dahl Selection *edited by* Hélène Fawcett
Scene Scripts Five Four television plays *edited by* Alison Leake
*****Race to be Seen** *edited by* Alison Leake and Mark Wheeller
Festival Plays *edited by* Margaret Mackey
Dash and Defiance *edited by* Alison Leake
Hear Me Out *compiled and edited by* Roy Blatchford
A Special Occasion Three plays *edited by* Alison Leake
The Diary of Anne Frank *edited by* Christopher Martin
Wishful Thinking selections from the writings of Keith Waterhouse
Intensive Care Four television plays *edited by* Michael Church
The Woman in Black Susan Hill
John Mortimer Plays Four plays *edited by* Mark Pattenden
Billy Liar Keith Waterhouse
Ghost Stories *selected by* Susan Hill
People Working *compiled and edited by* Maura Healy

*Cassette available

Acknowledgements

We are grateful to the following for permission to reproduce copyright material:

Chatto & Windus/The Hogarth Press for stories 'Andrina' by George Mackay Brown from *Andrina and other Stories* & 'The July Ghost' by A.S. Byatt from *Sugar and other Stories*; Authors' Agents for story 'A Kind of Swan Song' by Helen Cresswell. © Helen Cresswell 1984; Authors' Agents for story 'The Man Who Didn't Believe in Ghosts' by Sorche Nic Leodhas from *Ghosts Go Hunting* (Holt Rinehart). Copyright © 1965 by Le Clare G. Alger; Lutterworth Press for stories 'If She Bends, She Breaks' by John Gordon from *Catch Your Death* (Patrick Hardy Books) & 'The Darkness Under the Stairs' by Lance Salway from *The Darkness Under the Stairs* (1988 – Lutterworth); Methuen Children's Books for story 'The Sea Bride' by Vivien Alcock from *Ghostly Companions*; Penguin Books Ltd for story 'The Shadow-Cage' by Philippa Pearce from *The Shadow-Cage and other Stories of the Supernatural* (Kestral Books 1977). Copyright © Philippa Pearce, 1977; Authors' Agents on behalf of The Literary Executors of the Estate of H.G. Wells for story 'The Red Room' by H.G. Wells.

LONGMAN GROUP UK LIMITED,
Longman House, Burnt Mill, Harlow,
Essex CM20 2JE, England
and Associated Companies throughout the world.

© Longman Group UK Limited 1990

This edition first published 1990

Set in 11/13 point Baskerville, Linotron 202
Produced by Longman Singapore Publishers Pte Ltd
Printed in by Singapore

ISBN 0 582 02661 X